Anna Seghers
Crossing

A Love Story

DIÁLOGOS
An Imprint of Lavender Ink
DIALOGOSBOOKS.COM

Anna Seghers. *Crossing: A Love Story*
Anna Seghers. *Überfahrt. Eine Liebesgeschichte*
© Aufbau Verlag BmbH & Co. KG, Berlin 1971, 2008
Translated by Douglas Irving
English translation copyright © 2016 by Douglas Irving and Diálogos.
All rights reserved. No part of this work may be reproduced
in any form without the express written permission
of the copyright holders and Diálogos Books.

Printed in the U.S.A.
First Printing
10 9 8 7 6 5 4 3 2 1   16 17 18 19 20 21

Book and cover design: Bill Lavender
Back cover artwork: Ishy Walters

Library of Congress Control Number: 2015959064
Seghers, Anna
Crossing: A Love Story / Anna Seghers;
with Douglas Irving (translator)
p. cm.
Includes Introduction by Min Zhou
ISBN: 978-1-935084-94-5 (pbk.)

Other editions:
ISBN: 978-1-935084-96-9 (ebook)

DIÁLOGOS
AN IMPRINT OF LAVENDER INK
DIALOGOSBOOKS.COM

Acknowledgments

The Goethe poem referred to by its first line on page 128 is known in English by the title "The Wanderer's Nightsong II." A fine translation of the poem by John Whaley is displayed in Goethe's hut at the top of the Kickelhahn hill outside Ilmenau in Germany.

My warm thanks to the following people for their invaluable input to this translation: Daniel Martineschen, Jürgen Thomaneck, Jim Mellis, Ernest Schonfield, Genevieve Guzman, Patricia Nash, Livia Vonaesch, Judy Taylor, Ishy Walters, Karen McPhail, Gregor Campbell and Mary Irving.

On several occasions when translating Triebel's troubles I found inspiration in the song lyrics of transatlantic Scottish band Trashcan Sinatras, in particular their 2004 song "Weightlifting."

Finally, my thanks to Bill Lavender at Diálogos for editorial input, and for publishing this important late work of Anna Seghers in English translation.

Contents

Foreword by Min Zhou — vi

Crossing: A Love Story — 21

Biographical Notes — 161

Foreword

Min Zhou, Roger Williams University

Anna Seghers, author of *Crossing: A Love Story*, is considered "the greatest female German writer" of the twentieth century (Mayer 204). A member of the Communist Party of Germany since 1928 and of the East German governing party after her return from exile in 1947, Seghers was also a politically conscious and engaged writer (Schrade VII). It is thus little surprising that discussions of her literature often became denouncement or endorsement of her communist views and her political attitudes, even when one tried to examine her work from a literary perspective. The controversies over Seghers's literature reflect the disrupted world in which she lived (IX). Now that the Cold War has finally ended, archival material and many of Seghers's personal papers and documents released after the fall of the Berlin Wall in 1989 shed new light on her life and writing. It has thus become more important than before to read or re-read her literature, especially those works created under the East German regime that she once supported and that has now dissolved. With historical hindsight and less charged with ideological biases that have shadowed Seghers's reception for more than half a century, we may finally develop the intellectual sensibility and cultural competency to discover and appreciate the subtleties between the lines in her literature and to understand and embrace her complexities as a writer. Such sensibility and competency are critical, especially in today's world teeming with turmoil and conflicts of all kinds that are caused by our fear and intolerance of differences, be they racial, economic, cultural, or political.

Seghers was born Netty Reiling in 1900 in Mainz, Germany, to a wealthy and assimilated Jewish family. She made her literary debut in 1924, under the pseudonym Seghers, after the Dutch painter Hercules Seghers, one of Rembrandt's contemporaries. Her literary talent soon gained recognition. In 1928, the novel *Aufstand der Fischer von St. Barbara* (Revolt of the Fishermen of Santa Barbara) and the story "Grubetsch" won her the Kleist prize, a prestigious literary award in the Weimar Republic. The two works are representative of Seghers's literature in their engagement with social issues such as the oppression of marginalized individuals and groups, "particularly the poor and disenfranchised" (Romero), and their fight against oppression. Stylistically, the two works—with "hard-hitting sparse language and expressive imagery" (Romero)—are also characteristic of her writing. Yet contention about Seghers started with these early works. Members of the Community Party, which she joined in 1928, criticized her award-winning work for lacking "politic-ideological clarity" (Hilzinger 92) and for not being "Marxist" (Brandes 35).

Seghers indeed differed from many proletarian revolutionary writers who subscribed to realism and prioritized a work's social relevance over its literary quality. As "one of the greatest modernists of her time" (Fehervary 1), Seghers assimilated influences from expressionism, documentary literature, montage techniques, and interior monologue (Hilzinger 45). At the same time, she sought opportunities to expound her modernist approach and to advocate for an open attitude towards different styles of writing. During her exile in Paris

(1933-1940), for instance, Seghers corresponded with the Marxist critic, Georg Lukács. She questioned his acceptance of the Soviet view that realism is a mirror of the world and countered him with the argument that splinters of a mirror can also reflect a fragment of the world. What may look like "wild breaks in style, experiments, peculiar mixed forms," is, according to her, "a forceful attempt at a new content" (Zhou 159).

Seghers remained in Paris until Nazi Germany invaded northern France in 1940, at which time she fled with her husband and two children to Marseille in southern France and then set sail to Mexico, where she stayed from 1941 until her return to Germany in 1947. Seghers wove this experience of flight into *Transit*, a novel that captures the perils of war and the desperate plight of refugees from all over Europe who have no place to stay and nowhere to go. "The most beautiful" novel (Böll 254) of Seghers is also a modernist one with numerous mythic and literary allusions and a multi-layered complexity that invites multiple readings and interpretations. Given its ambitions, it is little wonder that Seghers's German colleagues at the publishing house in exile in Mexico rejected her manuscript. The novel was published first in Spanish translation, then in English translation by Little Brown in Boston in 1944.

The exile in France also produced Seghers's most famous novel, *The Seventh Cross*, printed first in English translation by the same American publisher in 1942. The novel presents an epic view of Germany under Hitler's rule. It portrays not only Nazis and opportunists, but also quiet, ordinary people who overcome fear and help one of seven fugitives from a concentration camp to escape to freedom (Romero). A "Book of the Month Club" selection in October 1942, *The Seventh Cross* became an American bestseller as well as a 1944 MGM film starring Spencer Tracy.

That the English translations of *Transit* and *The Seventh Cross* were both printed first in the United States is not coincidental. As a matter of fact, Seghers had hoped to immigrate to the States, one of the important centers for German exiles during the war, and she and her family landed at Ellis Island in 1941. However, they were not permitted even a temporary entry. As much later revealed, Seghers was labeled a "camouflaged communist" in her FBI file and so was not welcome to the States (Stephan 12). These political anxieties also impacted the Hollywood film version of *The Seventh Cross*, which portrays its main character as "politically nondescript" (Horak 121) and not the communist in Seghers's work.

This fear of communism in the States foreshadowed a war that started at the end of World War II. Shortly after Seghers's return from exile, the Cold War escalated and broke up the former anti-Hitler coalition in Germany. With the founding of two German states in 1949, Seghers was forced to choose between East Germany, consisting of the former Soviet occupation zone, and West Germany, consisting of the former American, British, and French occupation zones.

It was a very difficult decision. Despite her faith in communism, Seghers settled in West Berlin after her return. She hoped to influence Germans in both the Western and Soviet occupation zones with her literature and to travel freely to visit her children, now based in Paris, and her husband, who remained in Mexico. Seghers also knew about Soviet show trials and purges in the 1930s and was deeply disappointed with the Hitler-Stalin pact in 1939. Moreover, it must have become clear to her over the years that the comrades of her party had not really appreciated her work. However, as the Cold War shifted West German priorities from denazification to anti-communism, many former Nazis were reintegrated into their previous positions and into government. To Seghers, West Germany seemed to have returned to the old social structure that had instigated Nazism. Having experienced war, exile, and the loss of her mother in the Holocaust—Seghers's mother was deported to a concentration camp in Poland and disappeared there—Seghers was more resolved than ever in her commitment to help build a socialist and democratic Germany. Such a new Germany, she believed, was the only option to prevent Nazism from happening again.

In 1950, after residing in West Berlin for more than three years, Seghers moved to East Berlin, gave up her Mexican passport, and became a citizen of East Germany. From the 1950s until her death in 1983, she held important positions there, including president of the East German Writers' Union, and was made a prominent public figure to represent East Germany as an anti-fascist state and a "Kulturnation."

Gradually, though, Seghers also became disappointed with the East German government, which was eager to turn its back on the immediate past and called on its writers to focus on the construction of socialism in contemporary Germany. She was even more disillusioned by the growing gap between the socialist ideal and its reality in East Germany. Yet her voice to champion more artistic freedom and individual artists was rather moderate. Seghers almost never disagreed with her party in public, for fear that her actions could be abused by the other side of the Iron Curtain; in fact, at crucial moments in East German history when writers, artists, and intellectuals expected her to speak up and defend them, to their dismay, she "supported her party by either publicly defending or not publicly opposing its actions" (Romero). As revealed after the dissolution of East Germany, Seghers intervened behind the scenes to negotiate with politicians for writers and artists, but to little avail.

Because of Seghers's loyalty to her party, she was rejected in West Germany as a "bankrupt" poet (Reich-Ranicki 17). Out of ignorance or animosity (Schrade VIII), West German critics flatly dismissed her literature written after 1949 as "a love declaration… to Stalin" (Reich-Ranicki). What many critics of both West and East Germany failed to recognize at the time was the fact that, contrary to her public statements or silence as a cultural representative, Seghers as a writer was much more open and free-spirited. After several failed works about the East German construction of socialism from the late 1940s through the mid 1960s, Seghers's confidence in a socialist future started to dissipate. She increasingly laid her eyes on the continent across the Atlantic Ocean, returned to her beloved genre of storytelling, and resumed writing stories that are set in Latin American and Caribbean countries. *Crossing: A Love Story*, which was written in 1971, is one of the works from this period.

Often compared to *Transit*, *Crossing* shares with the novel from exile many characteristics, among them ambiguity and complexity. *Crossing* could be read as a love story, as a portrayal of contemporary history, or as a story about storytelling, about the poetics of storytelling (Wende 27). Intertwining a love story with political events, *Crossing* tells more than a story of love. It also vividly represents recent German history, such as the persecution of Jews, the immediate postwar events that led to German division, and the 1950s reconstruction in East Germany. The portrayal of Brazil and East Germany in *Crossing* is anything but a black-and-white narrative between evil capitalism and good socialism, as East and West German critics wanted to claim. The main character is skeptical of many aspects of life in East Germany, while his love for Brazil does not blind him from seeing many of its social problems. Seghers's depiction of the two countries is subtle, sophisticated, and multifaceted.

Crossing is also intriguing for its structure. Ernst Triebel, whose love story forms the center of *Crossing*, is not the actual narrator; rather, the novel's reader learns of the story second-hand, through Franz Hammer. While less present, Hammer's role is not restricted to listening and passing on Triebel's story, but he also reflects on his own feelings about Triebel and comments on his changing relations to the love story as a listener (Wende 34). Moreover, Hammer observes other passengers on board a Polish ship from Latin America to Europe and relates their stories in third-person narration. This skillful structure, with its multiple narrative perspectives, echoes the work of Joseph Conrad (1857-1924), one of the writers and artists alluded to in *Crossing*. A Polish-British novelist and short-story writer, Conrad favored indirect narration, multiple changes of perspective, and nested flashbacks, all of which reflected his disbelief in an objective representation of reality (39). By having one of *Crossing's* characters tell Conrad's life story, Seghers drew attention to this influential modernist and implicitly challenged the East German regime's dictate of socialist realism, which required writers and artists to portray life "objectively."

Among the issues that divided East and West German critics in their reception of *Crossing* is the optimistic ending: by telling his story, Triebel has worked through his struggles, made up his mind, and is looking forward to resuming his life in East Germany. A recent study of Seghers's manuscripts of *Crossing* reveals that this ending did not exist in the penultimate draft and that Seghers added the ending into the typescript by hand at the urging of her husband, a staunch communist who did not always influence Seghers's writing favorably and whose critical comments on *Crossing* and many other of Seghers's works are also preserved (Romero 149, Albrecht 212-6).

In a 1970 interview, an interviewer misquoted a sentence from *Transit* by saying, "what can be told has been overcome," to which Seghers replied, "it is remarkable that in the novel I am currently working on [referring to *Crossing*] another view prevails: one can overcome it better by telling it" (Albrecht 212). This modification captures Seghers's changed perception of the function of storytelling. As a storyteller in the most original sense, Seghers told fictions, tales she heard, and stories from her own life (Hilzinger 78). If telling his own story is therapeutic to Triebel because it gives him an opportunity for self-reflection and self-knowledge, then to Seghers, storytelling is existential. In the 1930s and 1940s, telling stories helped her come to terms with and overcome the plight of exile. In the postwar period, on the other hand, storytelling has increasingly become for her an act of creating a community, a critical public sphere (Janzen 175) where the reader and the author could effect some change and better deal with the shared disappointment and irresolvable frustrations then existing in East Germany. To accomplish this, Seghers struggled to maintain a critical position as a socially engaged author while continuing to work within the system (Janzen 177), however difficult it was. In her effort to strike a balance between her loyalty to the party and her commitment to art and freedom of artistic expression, Seghers always relied on her literature to show more than her public statements did and "repeatedly pleaded for attentive readers who would appreciate the many layers of her work" (Romero).

Throughout her life, Seghers was reticent about personal matters and insisted that what counts is the work, not the life of an author. While she expressed this view in response to biographical questions, it also well summarizes her legacy: what we as readers and critics should focus on is her work, and not her life, because her contributions are not in politics, but in the poetics of her literature. "Let's read her books!" pleaded Christa Wolf (1929-2011), Seghers's most prominent literary successor, on the occasion of Seghers's 75th birthday (144). Let's follow her plea, too.

Works Cited

Albrecht, Friedrich. "Zwischen zwei Welten. Zu Anna Seghers' Erzählung »Überfahrt«." *Argonautenschiff* 11 (2002): 202-16.

Böll, Heinrich. "Afterword. *Perils among False Brethren.*" *Transit.* Trans. Dargot Bettauer Dembo. New York: New York Review of Books, 2013. 253-57.

Brandes, Ute. *Anna Seghers.* Berlin: Colloquium Verlag, 1992.

Fehervary, Helen. *Anna Seghers: The Mythic Dimension.* Ann Arbor: University of Michigan Press, 2001.

Horak, Jan-Christopher. "The Other Germany in Zimmermann's *The Seventh Cross.*" *German Film and Literature: Adaptations and Transformations.* Ed. Eric Rentschler. New York: Methuen, 1986. 117-31.

Hilzinger, Sonja. *Anna Seghers.* Stuttgart, Philipp Reclam, 2000.

Janzen, Marike. "Between the Pedagogical and the Performative: Personal Stories, Public Narratives, and Social Critique in Anna Seghers's *Überfahrt.*" *The German Quarterly* 79 (2006): 175-91.

Mayer, Hans. *Der Turm von Babel: Erinnerung an eine Deutsche Demokratische Republik.* Frankfurt a. M.: Suhrkamp, 1993.

Reich-Ranicki, Marcel. "Nicht gedacht soll ihrer werden?" *Frankfurter Allgemeine.* 167, 21 July 1990.

—. *Zur Literatur der DDR.* München: Piper, 1974.

Romero, Christiane Zehl. "Anna Seghers." Encyclopedia. Web. 10 Dec. 2015. <http://jwa.org/encyclopedia/article/seghers-anna>.

—. *Anna Seghers: Eine Biographie 1947-1983.* Berlin: Aufbau, 2003.

Schrade, Andreas. *Anna Seghers.* Stuttgart and Weimar: J.B. Metzler, 1993.

Stephan, Alexander. *Anna Seghers im Exil: Essays, Texte, Dokumente.* Bonn: Bouvier Verlag, 1993.

Wende, Waltraud. "*Überfahrt* von Anna Seghers. Liebesgeschichte, Zeitporträt und Erzählung über das Erzählen." *Euphorion* 92 (1998): 25-46.

Wolf Christa. "Zum 75. Geburtstag von Anna Seghers." *Das dicht besetzte Leben: Briefe, Gespräche und Essay.* Ed. Angela Drescher. Berlin: Aufbau, 2003. 144.

Zhou, Min. "Lu Xun, Peking Opera and Modernism: China as a Literary Model in Anna Seghers's 'Zwei Briefe über China'." *Colloquia Germanica* 41 (2008): 155-74.

Note:

The Roger Williams University Foundation to Promote Scholarship and Teaching has provided me with valuable time to write this foreword. I would like to thank Peter Thompson for guidance and John Madritch for comments and proofreading.

—Min Zhou

Anna Seghers
Crossing
A Love Story

"There's nothing like departure. No arrival, no reunion. You leave a part of the earth behind you for good. And whatever joy and pain you encountered there, once the gangway is raised, ahead of you lie three clear weeks at sea."

I said nothing to my young travel companion; he was probably just thinking aloud. I had known him all of twenty minutes. I had waited in line behind him at the document check where I established that he, like me, would leave our Polish ship, the *Norwid*, in Rostock. He was a doctor (a fact I likewise established at the document check) specializing in internal medicine and taking separate courses in tropical medicine, which explained why he had attended a conference in Bahia. The purser nodded indifferently, without objection.

What seemed to please my fellow passenger—the long sea journey ahead—didn't appeal to me. I would gladly have seen my family again as soon as possible. But I was booked. I had come by plane. The repair job—the reason for my trip to Rio Grande do Sul—had been straightforward. Senhor Mendez, who purchased the farm machinery from my company last year, shook his head in astonishment at our reliability when I appeared at his ranch four weeks after he lodged his complaint, according to contract. You see, my colleagues back home knew I had left with my wife and two little girls for the Tatra Mountains, but they had no qualms summoning me via telegram, hardly had our holiday begun—although they were at fault for leaving the machinery outside in the first place.

In addition my boss appealed to my conscience. I was near Prague so I could get on the next plane. He phoned to say I owed it to our state to fly to Brazil at once so that our foreign clients knew our republic strictly adhered to its contracts.

But all this meant nothing to the young man standing beside me. He struck me as rather odd. There is no need to suddenly tell a stranger what is going through your head.

"All these people on board," he mused, "all these people on land who still insist on shouting to each other! Look at them waving, crumpling their tear-soaked handkerchiefs! And I, I'm proud that no one exists here anymore for me to say goodbye to. Once the gangway is raised, everything will be over at last."

"Why don't they raise it?"

"Because they're still loading cargo. Do you see the crane over there? There's the grabber heading out again. It's loading a few more crates onto our ship. Look: there's the cook taking charge of the delivery. At the last minute he probably purchased everything left at the local market cheaply: papaya, guava, oranges, bananas, pineapple, avocado—the fruits of this country."

"I hope he's saved us some winter apples as well; for our last week, in preparation for home."

"I know this cook. He was here on my last journey, one that also had to be by sea. I sailed on the *Joseph Conrad*. I was looking after a delicate cargo on that occasion. This cook is a very thrifty individual. I'd wager he once ran an inn somewhere on the Baltic."

Meanwhile, what we had awaited took place: the gangway was raised. The pilot ship led us out of the harbor, between ships big and small hailing from every country in the world. "Then it will leave us to the ocean," the young man said in that tone of his, as though everything he had to impart was important; "the pilot ship will play no further part in our fate, on its way to guide another ship out and another one after that…." He broke off suddenly. "Excuse me, my name is Ernst Triebel."

"Franz Hammer. I'm an engineer," I said.

"I'm a doctor. That is, I've just completed my studies."

The shipmate rang the gong for lunch. As our ship was transporting cargo (coffee, to Poland and the German Democratic Republic), only a few cabins were reserved for passengers.

We quickly took our seats around two tables. The captain, first officer and first engineer were seated at a third. Behind a pillar I noticed another little table for a single lady, a sturdy nun warmly dressed in brown. She must have stipulated the right to take her meals alone. Apparently the thin elderly lady in the long skirt at my own table was her companion, because she frequently stood to slip behind the pillar and ask the nun if she needed anything. I was nearest her place at the head of the table so could easily watch her movements. Next to me, another passenger had his arm in a sling. But it didn't seem to spoil his good mood. His sharp, bright blue eyes darted from one passenger to the next. It quickly emerged he spoke Polish, German, Portuguese, Spanish, French and English (and the devil only knows what else). Abruptly, he turned his head and introduced himself: "Sadowski." Without further ado he bade me fill his plate with food and cut it up. He told me he had dislocated his arm while helping someone with luggage after boarding. The second officer (who also acted as the ship's doctor, since small ships like ours didn't have a dedicated one) had reset his arm there and then.

"It needs to heal by our arrival," Sadowski said. "I'm a technician. Got a job lined up in Gdynia. I've battled with myself for ten years: should I go home? I'd like to see my mother again while she's still alive. And now this bad luck in the first five minutes."

Not only did he speak every language known to man, he had already familiarized himself with the other passengers' stories, because then he said: "Turn round a moment, discreetly; at the other table, directly behind you, there's a wrinkled old lady who spent decades in Brazil. She arrived with the Polish family who cried themselves half to death saying goodbye. She looked after this family's children from infancy right up to marriage. And to show their gratitude the family let her take home all the rubbish they no longer need: three generations' worth of woolens. Her employers probably got rich in Brazil. But they told her the things they were throwing out were necessary for our arctic Poland."

Turning to the next table, I caught sight of the old lady. She wore a blue wool hat. My eyes also rested on Triebel. He signaled to me: *later*.

"The nun in brown, the Carmelite, only stayed in Brazil for a few weeks," Sadowski said. "Did you not come with her from Bahia? She stayed at her order's sumptuous house. She's probably smuggled a whole load of our money."—He was already saying "our"—"A party of pretty, pious girls flocked around her with going-away presents. Not nuns but children, too young to wed either an earthly or heavenly bridegroom."

He turned to speak in Polish to the blonde-plaited girl on his other side. The mother, also blonde, sat between her daughter and her son. *I bet this Sadowski already knows why they're on the ship*, I thought. And I was envious that he had spent year after year in this corner of the world and lost nothing of his mother tongue. *Neither would I*, I thought then: *you never lose your own language*.

Before long, Sadowski revealed what he knew about these people. The father was a consular official whose children attended a Brazilian school in Rio. The mother gave them Polish lessons. Their suitcases were filled with Polish schoolbooks. Before the holidays ended she was taking the children home to sit their exams in Krakow. When the father returned home for good they could receive training in any profession they pleased.

I offered the lady my compliments. Only perseverance allowed bilingual learning, I said. Sadowski relayed my compliments. The lady looked a little stern. But her face lit up with pleasure at my praise.

We were served our dessert, pineapple, prepared as is usual in this country, the fruit first scooped out so that something like a boat sits on the plate, the flesh cut into little pieces and the shell, the boat on the plate, filled with these.

That's too much trouble for our cook, I thought. *Let's see how long he keeps it up.*

The unassuming old lady at the head of the table didn't touch her pineapple. She took it directly to the nun in brown, who cheerfully thanked her and instantly began to eat. The couple opposite me were whispering. I assumed their intention of offering pineapple to this nun had proved unnecessary. Whereupon both began to greedily eat theirs and then scrape out the shells.

Sadowski whispered to me that the small round husband was a famous singer in Poland. Just now he had given guest performances in Rio and São Paulo. Sadowski had been at the Rio concert. The entire Polish expat community wept, he said. The singer had sung nothing contemporary, no heart-rending songs, instead opting for old heart-warming hymns, as well as poems newly set to music—like some by Norwid. He asked if I knew of him.

"No, never heard of him," I replied.

"That's a shame. Even I know of him, and I'm just an electrician. Our ship's named after him. You must know of Joseph Conrad though, surely?"

I didn't dare say no again, that back in the GDR these writers weren't very well known. I quickly considered my excuse. Since I didn't read a lot, perhaps I had simply not heard of him. So I said: "Yes, of course."

"Many people," Sadowski said, "think that Conrad was an Englishman. But he was Polish. He became a sailor and left for England."

"Why?" I asked. In my ignorance I imagined the man may have left his country to settle in the West, like so many others.

But Sadowski continued, "Joseph Conrad was obsessed with ships. Back then Poland didn't yet have access to the sea. He first saw the sea and met naval officers when traveling with his private tutor and that settled it for him. His whole life—whether on board or on land—he wrote novels set at sea. Incidentally, he never stopped loving Poland, even while in England."

I resolved to purchase one of Joseph Conrad's books upon my arrival (if we actually printed him). "Joseph Conrad would be delighted now because we have a substantial stretch of sea," Sadowski said.

It struck me how oddly proud this man Sadowski was of his stretch of sea; yet he had spent years wondering whether he should return to Poland.

I retired to my cabin after lunch. The man I shared it with had eaten behind me at the other table. Now he lay on his bed and stared at me in silence. My appearance irritated him. Everyone had been friendly during the meal, but the angry silence written on his face said: whether from Rostock or Frankfurt, you murdered my brothers. I couldn't speak Polish and besides couldn't barge in and inform him my father had been killed by Nazis in a concentration camp. In any case, I was a child in the war and had never even seen Poland. Explaining to him why I was sailing on a Polish ship would have involved a long speech he wouldn't have understood.

As he didn't stop scowling I quickly left the cabin. I went on deck. A glimmer of coastline was still visible. My young fellow traveler, Ernst Triebel, stood where I had met him that morning. Contrary to what he had said about "farewells", he gazed ceaselessly at the strip of coastline, perhaps now no more than fog. Gulls (or whatever seabirds were called here) circled above us. They could still fly back.

"Were you at the industrial trade fair in São Paulo?"

"I didn't have time. I had this urgent repair to see to in Rio Grande do Sul. So urgent I flew over by plane. And now I'm returning on the Polish ship that happened to be sailing at this time."

"So that's how it was with you," Ernst Triebel said; "with me it was different."

"No doubt. It's different with everyone."

"In my case, especially so."

"Everyone thinks their case is special somehow."

"There are certain things that are hard to bear. In my case, I've scarcely borne them. Now, when I think how quiet the next few weeks will be, I feel that this special thing may fade. It may fade, but that's not yet certain. I'm not even sure if it *should* fade—from memory, I mean."

"Do you really think all these birds will fly home?"

"All of them. I know they will. This is now my third trip. The first time I sailed to Brazil as a little boy with my parents on the North German Lloyd Shipping Line. Two years ago I sailed from Gdynia to Santos. This time I came by plane, but I have to return by boat—probably for the last time."

"You can't be sure about that. I certainly can't, if my work has some other assembly in this country. It may be the same for you, too." I had the feeling that the young man now needed to say what was on his mind.

"The first time we traveled here shortly before *Kristallnacht*, if you know what that is."

"Yes, yes, of course. I learnt about it at school—something bad with the Jews." I was pleased I had been able to answer him more quickly than I had Sadowski his questions about Joseph Conrad.

"My father wasn't a Jew," Triebel said, "but he was afraid of being separated from my mother. He loved her a great deal. It was lucky that her brother already lived in Rio then and had sent us visas and tickets."

"Was your mother beautiful?"

"When my father finally made the decision to leave, I think I saw her properly for the first time. She resembled the women and girls from *One Thousand and One Nights*. I suddenly understood why my father chose to go far away for her sake. His love wasn't only about that, though. Love dwells deep inside you, yet remains connected to something visible. That's what makes love special. Do you know what I mean?"

"The seagulls are still there, though you can no longer see the coast."

"They probably come from the large island of Fernando de Noronha. Our ship sails past it in the night. The Brazilians imprison their criminals there."

That moment, a bright young man came springing down

the steps toward us.

"Günter Bartsch, my neighbor at dinner," Triebel said.

Exuding enthusiasm and energy, the boy said more to Triebel than to me, "Come on up. You can already see a bit of the island on the radar."

The passengers were already standing in a queue: the singer, Sadowski, the incensed Pole from my cabin, the nun, the nanny in the blue hat, the consul's wife and her two children, perhaps a few others I didn't know, and now the young man Günter Bartsch, Triebel, and I. An officer focused the radar, explaining in Polish. One by one we peered at patch with indents on the luminous glass.

I had never looked through a radar before. I only knew that someone had to monitor it so the ship didn't hit a rock or an island.

"The Italian steamer disaster occurred because the iceberg was too close to steer the ship away," Sadowski informed us. "The captain will never be allowed to take the helm again—although the ship's officer was most at fault; he wasn't monitoring the radar. He was with his colleague, the telegraph operator. No one suspected the iceberg to go so deep. All this first came to light in the maritime court."

After watching the indented patch on the bright background, Triebel and I went down on deck. The real island materialized in the evening haze. After dinner, we sailed past a rocky promontory. It seemed that the island moved out of our way, only to drift back in again. Lights twinkled in gaps in the hills.

Night fell. I was finding the cabin too stuffy, so after a few hours I got up and went on deck. Triebel was standing in his old spot as though he had never left it. I watched him. He was gazing at the fast disappearing vestiges of island, now barely visible, as though it pained him.

"That was the last piece of America," he said, adding softly, as one speaks to a sick child (only he was speaking to himself), "when we see the lighthouse at Brittany we'll be in Europe. In between is sea: three weeks." He no longer appeared as wildly enthusiastic about these three entirely free weeks at sea.

"When you traveled to Rio for the first time did you sail past the island too?" I asked, merely to distract him from whatever weighed on him.

"Probably," he said tiredly. "I was still a child and didn't pay attention. The ship was packed with émigrés. Father and Mother mostly spoke intensely with each other. They must have been comforting one another. They simply couldn't take in the departure. We were four in the cabin. Apart from the three of us, there was another older boy who taught me to play chess.

"At the time my uncle—my mother's brother, whom I didn't know—was deputy director of a tuberculosis sanatorium not far from Rio.

"Upon arrival we stared at the colossal, cacophonous city. We might have fared badly if my uncle hadn't appeared as we disembarked. He kissed my mother but greeted my father rather coldly; he had long since forgotten their time studying together. I think he patted me on the shoulder.

"All at once I feared my uncle, although he was a doctor like any other. I also realized laws prevailed here that undermined everything. Time itself was subject to such a law. For instance, until today I honestly hadn't thought of the boy in the cabin with us who taught me to play chess.

"I held on tight to my mother. My uncle went with us to customs. It's called *alfândega*, an Arabic word. In Rio it's an enormous hall teeming with new arrivals and their luggage. The black people amazed me most, and the hordes of monks. They had probably just left their Italian ship. Amid so many languages, theirs rang out like a bell.

"We quickly got our luggage because my uncle spoke Portuguese like a Brazilian and was fairly forthright.

"Then we ate somewhere. My uncle, in charge now, revealed (not as a suggestion but a gentle order) that he would drive with my parents to this sanatorium. That was where my father would work. He said there was a room for Father and Mother. Me, on the other hand, he'd take to the excellent English boarding school that his sons also attended. He said it would be unbelievably hard to find a place at a better school here. But he had been lucky; the head of the school, a Mrs. Whittaker, had accepted his sons, he told us. 'And now she's going to accept you too, little man, because I'm treating her son on an on-going basis, so up to a point she's depending on me.'

"When my mother asked shyly: 'Can he not come with us? Stay in our room?' my uncle said dismissively: 'Impossible.'

"All three of us were stunned. Then he added: 'Have you not read the papers? Better thank God you're here at all. Don't be picky, Hanna.'

"What could we have done? The little building my uncle drove us to looked clean and tidy. Mrs. Whittaker greeted us icily. I wept bitterly when my mother kissed me goodbye.

I remember remaining in the empty dormitory during the evening meal.

"Perhaps a dozen boys stayed in our room, including one of my cousins. But my cousins treated me as an outsider. They often made fun of me because I could speak neither English nor Portuguese. I kept wondering when my mother would visit again. She came after a few days. We were both happy. Shortly afterwards, something happened that changed my childhood. Do you mind if I quickly tell you about it?"

I had a strong feeling that he needed to keep talking, so I said, "No, no. Please tell me everything."

Twilight flooded the sea. Two currents mingled, one already inky blue from the stars' reflection, the other luminous and restless, perhaps still awash with island foam. The ship's swaying created a steady interchange of sky and sea before our eyes. I would much rather have reveled in it silently, without words, without voices, but Ernst Triebel carried on, "I waited a long time for my mother to visit again, in vain. She wrote a few times, saying that she was ill. One day, my father appeared. I saw at once by his face what had happened. He led me out onto the street. We walked up and down and then sat on an empty bench. We were silent. Finally my father said: 'It was a severe case of typhoid—she caught an infection!'

"'So she is no longer alive,' I said.

"'She is no longer alive,' my father said, and rather than comfort me (the thought never entered his head), there and then he poured out his heart, as though I was now grown up. And as he outlined his and my future, a very dark-skinned mulatto man, or was it a black man, sat down on our bench. I can still clearly remember the man. He was practicing a strange instrument I'd never seen before. It was as though his melody accompanied my father's sad but decisive words. My father said that, after Mother's death, nothing in the world would make him stay on at this sanatorium. Neither would he tolerate living under the same roof as his brother-in-law. He told me my mother had suffered greatly during the short time. He said she had been ashamed of her brother. Even before she fell ill they had decided to move to Rio and live there unaided somehow.

"'Because, you see, I still have some savings,' my father said. 'As luck would have it,' he continued, 'a kind patient revealed to me that a small clinic is starting up here in the city.'

The head of the new practice told my father he would be glad of a fine German doctor—although in actual fact he couldn't legally employ him. Therefore he would register him as one of the nursing staff. He admitted that he couldn't immediately pay my father a registered doctor's salary.

"'But my new boss is friends with a headmaster,' my father said, 'and I've stipulated that this friend accepts you, my boy, into his school. You know how hard it is to be accepted into a good school here. Mind you, you'll have to learn Portuguese from scratch.'

"That's how it was, you understand, in the first six months after our arrival."

I found it strange that young Triebel felt such a strong need to tell me his memories. Memories that went back many years.

"Something extremely important happened to me at this school," Ernst Triebel said; "the special thing we spoke about first entered in. I mean it began there. It only ended yesterday, no, the evening before yesterday. This must be our second day at sea now?"

"Our second day."

"We've enough time for storytelling," Triebel added: "almost three weeks." All the same, as though we were in a hurry we started to walk round and round the locked cargo holds, even though I would have happily contemplated the star-sparkled sea.

As we went, Triebel continued to tell me the thing he had to get off his mind, as though not just the journey freed him to an extent, but also this ceaseless walking, and in me, his countryman, he might have found the listener who perhaps even understood the strange thing that he himself hadn't yet begun to understand and that only through telling it would.

All at once the sun arose. Though it wasn't yet ablaze, sky and sea shone golden and red and everything felt fresh, intent on happiness, I too.

"I found it hard at the new school," Triebel said, "although the teacher must have been gentle on me, as instructed by the headmaster. For a long time I couldn't understand Portuguese. The teacher wasn't angry; however, he was as disheartened as me. We both thought I would never learn the language. And as he said as much and gave me back my jotter in which the mistakes outnumbered the words—despite me having agonized for days and nights over the assignment—all at once I was in despair.

"There was an ugly old roofed area for rubbish bins in the schoolyard. Rats sometimes scurried around there. A class punishment was to take the wastebasket there to empty. I, though, went over there now to have a good cry, my back to the yard. For the first time I had a proper cry. I realized I wasn't just crying about the mistakes in my assignment—I felt I was doomed. 'You won't get anywhere here without Portuguese,' my father often said. I was crying because suddenly here we were in Brazil; I was crying over my mother because she died just after our arrival, her tenderness was gone. Where was she? I would also die but would I then go to be with her? At home my father once said that was just superstition. My father was a stolid, almost a hard person. Even the comfort he gave was hard.

"I squeezed myself between the bins and cried and cried. All at once someone touched my hair, someone said to me in German: 'Why are you crying?' I turned my puffed face around. I was looking at a girl from my class. I had probably seen her before but immediately forgotten her again; I had taken her to be Brazilian. But she proceeded to say to me in German: 'I needed a whole year to understand Portuguese. Suddenly it clicked—reading and writing too. It was like a miracle. It'll be the same for you too. If you like, Ernesto, we can study together a little every day. You see, I'm glad to be able to speak German with someone. And I bet you know stories and poems too. I don't want to forget a word. Shall I help you? Yes? Do you want to help me? Yes? So I don't forget my German?'

"She wiped my eyes with her pinafore. After a few more sobs I stopped crying. What she said sounded good."

He walked faster, my new young friend Triebel, and I followed him so as not to miss a word. At first I had only been half listening. Now I was all ears.

"The girl was called Maria Luisa Wiegand. 'I have to quickly buy some fruit and vegetables,' she said after school. 'My aunt's having visitors. I'm an orphan. I live with my Aunt Elfriede. Everything's similar with us, only both my parents died: my mother back home when I was little and my father from an illness here in Rio. And since I've known Aunt Elfriede from little, perhaps things aren't quite as hard for me. Now then, do you want to study at mine? I have to go shopping now.'

"She took me to a small market where she picked out fruit with great care: four mangos, golden half-moons I'd never eaten before. She turned each one in the air and made sure they weren't bad; avocados—I'd never eaten these before either. But she said she would make a delicious dish from them and let me have a taste. And two or three more kinds of fruit I didn't know. Lastly she bought coffee and sweets, saying: 'The guest shouldn't see we're poor. My aunt does crochet work and sews blouses. She runs one of the small shops on the Rua Catete.'

"I carried everything back to her front door. The hall was narrow as a hosepipe, the stairs steep. It was like squeezing yourself through a mine. Afterwards, when I saw how narrow the house front was, it was incredible to think how many floors and apartments were inside.

"We only lived twenty minutes away on a side street, Father and I. Our apartment was by no means big either. I slept in the same room as my father. We could barely fit our luggage in the next room, but I arranged the suitcases so they formed a sort of desk I studied at when my father had visitors.

"I would just like to say I always got on well with my father. He was generous and fair.

"Because we stayed in a rear apartment we had quick access to the big yard. It was full of shrubs and flower beds. The front of the building gave onto the street.

"The next day, Maria Luisa brought us a selection of the sweets we had purchased. Then I went back with her. She let me lick the remains of the avocado dish. I was amazed how many rooms this apartment had. It was as deep as it was narrow. There was one tiny room after another. Both Maria and her aunt had a separate room.

"The girl enjoyed coming to ours to study and do assignments; most of all because of the big windows overlooking the yard with its many shrubs and flowers. We split our study time, either at hers or at mine, as we felt like. I made good progress with Maria Luisa's help.

"We were never apart from the first day we met. Before long I could speak and write Portuguese. We read a book, *The Mulatto* (which I found gruesome). We reflected upon the book and everything around us: God and heaven, life and death. We always went shopping together. Sometimes we ate at her Aunt Elfriede's. Sometimes we surprised my father with an unusual Brazilian meal. He was always pleased when she prepared a pineapple for him like they do locally, or her special avocado dish. He took an instant shine to the girl. 'Who would believe she's from Thuringia?' he said. 'She's as lovely, lithe and golden brown as some girls in this city.'

"There really was a gleam of gold in her skin, such that you hardly saw the real white.

"We often went to the beach together. To begin with she could swim better than me, but I caught her up. Lots of men winked at her or shouted a word to her. She just shook her wet hair, smiling.

"That this girl possessed something which shone as much within her as without—the shimmer that we call beauty, a kind of beauty that even makes miserable people marvel, gives them cause for hope—of course I didn't yet know that at the time.

"Sometimes on the train someone suddenly spoke to her, but she just smiled and shook her head. When I asked her what the man had wanted, she replied: 'Nothing special. He just said I was pretty.'

"I didn't care if someone said something like that to her. I was glad I had found such a lovely companion.

"At school and after school, our lives were such that we were never apart, whether reading, studying, shopping or swimming. At the time we thought this was our portion in life; that we would invariably be together everywhere, always and forever."

That week they showed a film. We had to go down into the bowels of our ship. We all stared at the film unrolling under the sea, including the nun. Ernst Triebel stayed on deck with Günter Bartsch. They were studying the sky. That bright cheery boy had an amazing knowledge of the stars.

"They'll only show boring films that don't upset anyone, particularly not the Germans; because Germany caused Poland such terrible suffering in the war," Sadowski said.

The film was set in the Middle Ages on one of the amber trade routes. Along the way you saw the old towns from the

Baltic Sea down to the Mediterranean. At one of the inns where the convoy always stopped, a girl was in love with a merchant. I think the passengers were bored. With my fairly hard job as an engineer, always on the road, I enjoyed watching what went on in the Middle Ages, in the film unrolling underwater. Under the sea I watched what happened on earth in the Middle Ages.

My cabin mate, whom I rarely saw by day (he sat behind me at Triebel's table), was also in the audience. He didn't come up to our cabin afterwards. A few hours later, I awoke because he had smashed something and was making a real racket. He had drunk plenty in the interim. He often drank. At first I didn't know with whom, then I realized: with Sadowski. But it didn't bother him, whether little or lots. Either way, Woytek was being particularly noisy tonight. Eventually I jumped up and grabbed hold of him and threw him on his bed, and when he still wasn't quiet I chucked him out. I don't know whether he then had more to drink or slept somewhere. In any case, two sailors brought him back in the morning and laid him on his bed and he slept like a log, not even waking up for breakfast.

"Do you know why he drinks so much?" Sadowski asked. That morning I was walking up and down on deck with him instead of with Triebel.

I laughed. "Because he's a drunk. Any secret there?"

"Of course. Always, when someone drinks. I know why he does it, the poor guy."

"Namely?"

"You've got it into your head he's angry with you because you're a German, because they killed his brother. It's quite otherwise with him: when war broke out he sailed to England as first officer. The man who is now our captain was then second officer on the same ship. Our captain's a brave man. He stayed with his fleet in England. He took munitions to Murmansk. You know, out of the ten ships on that mission, at least six were destroyed. The second officer was lucky. He returned to Poland after the war and eventually became captain on the *Norwid*. But in London, Woytek from your cabin was offered the chance to make a lot of money. A person isn't simply brave, right? They're always brave for something specific. But whatever show of bravery this Woytek might have been capable of, the good offer, the promise of the high life far outweighed it.

"He took over a company in Recife. Recife's almost on the equator. You were in Rio Grande do Sul? There they talk of Recife and Fernambuco as being in the north.

"Hopefully the company I'm joining for my dear old mother's sake needs someone to go to South America now and then," he continued, somewhat gloomily. "You're lucky they got sloppy and left your ranchero's combine harvester out in the open."

How had the wise guy heard that? I wondered.

"Anyway, your cabin mate went bankrupt in Recife. Maybe initially he did quite well. He got drunk, but no sailor put him to bed. He lay out on some street in the equatorial sun and by the time he was barely half-awake he'd had it. Maybe he made it to a hospital. In any event, his business went kaput because his wife, a black woman, didn't really know how to run it.

"He was in such a bad way that in the end the Polish embassy sent him home under pressure from the Brazilian government. And as he gets on this ship, who does he see? The captain, who was his second officer on the journey to England that time. And he, Woytek, he's now a nothing and our captain's a magnificent captain. That's why Woytek's starting to drink again and do really daft things. Hasn't a thing to do with you. I think he does it because he's ashamed."

"At home someone like that soon gets knocked into shape," I said.

"Hmm," said Sadowski.

I bet there's plenty knocking to be done in his case as well, I thought. But he said quite calmly: "It must feel strange being sent home at the consulate's expense like a hopeless loser, a good-for-nothing, and your ship's captain was once your subordinate, to boot."

Whatever the case, it was no pleasure for me to go back to my cabin to find this Woytek either half or completely drunk, or full to bursting with verbal venom.

He remained entirely in the dark as to the changes that had taken place in the world since his sunstroke. He hadn't taken in the division of Germany or that in the east a new German state had emerged which was now at peace with Poland. Maybe he did drink out of shame. However, his shame was projected directly onto me.

I had no reason to be ashamed. I never knew the war. I was still at school when I was briefly made a flak helper. My oldest brother, he was killed in action. We were all fond of him, which is why to this day none of us have got over his death. My sister had a bad leg so avoided the League of German Girls. I cannot say what my poor brother did before he fell at the Eastern Front. I only know that someone at my engineering works told us how his own son came home one day, as though out of his mind: "You parents, you never told us what you did to the Russians, the Czechs, the Polish, the French and the other nations. Now you go on about this imperialism that you yourselves are caught up in.

"It was you who brought it about, this imperialism. You should have told us everything, you really should have. Now we are the ones who feel remorse, because you feel none. We feel joint guilt. We feel joint remorse." My work colleague told us this during the break, and one colleague said: "Young folk nowadays ask all these questions that you just can't answer." But another one said: "You should have given him a slap," whereupon the others shouted at him: "You're crazy. He would have been locked up."

I was glad I had been too young for this war.

I wouldn't have minded discussing with Woytek his thoughts in my cabin. He wasn't up to it. I already said he was stuck in his pre-sunstroke period. The phrase "so we feel joint remorse for you" would never have entered his head. I found the idea appealing. I have only ever heard of compassion, but joint remorse—this boy had invented that.

I didn't like to speak about such things with Ernst Triebel either. When I appeared on deck he usually started to talk about Maria Luisa, and at first I listened bored, then willingly, until finally I was gripped.

"We never had any secrets, Maria Luisa and I. We spoke about everything under the sun, including Vargas, who was president at the time. I told her that one night during our crossing a Brazilian steamer sailed past us.

"'Maybe Prestes's wife, who Vargas handed over to Hitler, was on that very ship,' she exclaimed.

"'How would you know that?'

"'You hear everything here,' she shrugged. I listened to what she knew about this man called Prestes. She told me he walked across the country with a crowd of unemployed farm workers that steadily grew from farm to farm. When I told my father, he said: 'All true. Only you shouldn't talk aloud about such things.'"

Even now, staring into the water Triebel told me something else. "In class they often asked me: 'Is she still a young girl?' I evaded the question, as though I hadn't understood it."

Why does Triebel tell me such a thing? I asked myself. And at the same time I thought of the answer: *because he wouldn't tell it anywhere else but here on the ship.* Then I thought again: *It's quiet all around us. Triebel needs this place. You need a place, in order to tell a person everything.*

"Around this time, after us having previously spent every spare minute together, Maria suddenly started to make different friends. She explained nothing and I asked nothing. She simply said: 'We can't go to the beach this afternoon. I promised Eliza I'd go to the concert with her.'

"There was nothing wrong in that. Eliza was a girl from our class, unattractive but strong-willed. She was determined to study music. As her family obviously wasn't short of a penny, she had been having private piano lessons for a long time. Maria sometimes went round to hers and would then tell me how wonderfully this girl played. 'Not only will she be a music teacher,' Maria said, 'but a famous artist in her own right.'

"I felt a pang, I don't quite know why, when Rodolfo, a boy from our class, claimed that his mother was of the same opinion, and she knew a lot about music. It emerged during such conversations that Maria, together with Eliza, were sometimes guests of Rodolfo's family.

"One day, when I had scoured the beach in vain for Maria but only spotted Eliza at a distance with Rodolfo's youthful, well-dressed mother, I ran up to Marias aunt's. There you go: Maria was at home all alone. She was glad I had come. She said she suddenly hadn't felt like swimming anymore. 'Eliza and Rodolfo's mother are sitting at a café on the beach,' I said. 'Well, let them,' Maria replied.

"Sometimes Maria Luisa seemed changed, although I couldn't have said what the change was. Once, she took my face in her hands, looked me in the eyes and said: 'You are and will remain my only friend on earth.'

"She kissed me. I didn't dare properly kiss her back. I stroked her hair and her arms.

"Regarding this change that I sometimes noticed in her, or only thought to notice, it was also that her face was no longer as trusting, but proud and secretive. Her smile had grown bold, as though she was proud of something that had befallen her. She held herself very straight. Her chest was firm. With her flowing, golden brown hair and her sun-browned face, she looked lovelier than ever.

"Aunt Elfriede had a housemaid called Odilia.

"We had read the book *The Mulatto* again, far more carefully, far more consciously than before. And one morning, as Odilia was cleaning the apartment, Maria Luisa asked her point-blank what it had been like under slavery, whether she too had experienced such a thing; whether it was true that slaves were sold. Horrified, Odilia in turn asked how she had come upon such a thing. From a book? She said it must be an awful book if it recalled such times. Yes, certainly her mother had been a slave, but she didn't have it bad, she said. Her job had been to look after her owners' vegetable garden and these owners, mostly in North America, hadn't made a fuss when she, Odilia, was born into the world during this time, in fact they hardly noticed.

"By this time a law existed according to which children of slaves went free. So she, Odilia, was never a slave herself on account of this law, she told us.

"However, shortly before this definitive law of freedom (called the 'Golden Law'), something bad happened to her mother and consequently to her as well: a letter arrived from the United States that said the nice owners weren't coming back. As a result, the house and garden were sold off into the hands of cruel, greedy people.

"'My mother was still a slave at this point,' Odilia told us, 'and I was free. This made these people, the new owners, furious. Why should they pay for a child to skip and dance, and feed it over and above? Because there were constant arguments and threats my mother decided to send me somewhere else. She found a job for me at a market. Granted it was quite far away. At first I slept out in the open, then under a fruit cart. I only saw my mother a few times a year because, despite her efforts to keep her job for my sake, she was sold to a friend of the housewife in another city. The Golden Law wasn't yet valid (just make a quick profit while people could still be sold). But eventually one night my mother came to see me and said there was a position free near to her in the city. I went there at once, before daybreak. From this position, which didn't greatly appeal, I soon went to work for your aunt.'

"But then out of the blue Aunt Elfriede dismissed this Odilia, the daughter of a slave, for a reason Maria Luisa told me about much later on, shortly before my departure.

"Not far from our apartments there was a street cobbler by the name of Theodosio, who mended all manner of shoes from Maria's family and mine in his little booth. He was a black man. You saw straightaway that he was an intelligent person with good powers of observation. He regularly read the newspaper. He often smoothed out old newspapers that the shoes were wrapped in. He found this and that article which he carefully kept aside. He hadn't managed to set up a shop, just this stall which, if a storm threatened or he went away, he took down and then put back up. He asked Maria Luisa about school and asked us to show him our books and was pleased if we let him have an old jotter to look at, or even a book.

"To our amazement this clever young man began a friendship with Odilia, the aunt's housemaid. At first we couldn't tell what kind of relationship it was.

"Odilia was far older, she was completely uneducated, perhaps had never even felt the need of an education. Given that Theodosio was not unfriendly towards her (Maria thought he was a long way from starting a relationship; that he was as friendly with everyone anyway), Odilia, used to rudeness and ridicule, was for her part head-over-heels in love. We children noticed that Odilia sought every opportunity to pop by the cobbler's booth. Then we didn't give their friendship any more thought.

"Perhaps a month later I was going up to Maria's apartment; that morning we had decided to check each other's homework. We were studying a fair bit at the time; an exam loomed. Maria Luisa had borrowed some key texts from our classmate Rodolfo (not even we had enough money to buy all the necessary books). The books were heavy, and Rodolfo had handed them in at Aunt Elfriede's.

"Even on the stairs I heard the aunt's angry voice. I shuddered; such was the severity of the woman's rage. Her wrath seemed to increase by the second.

"She was still cursing when finally she opened the door. I saw at once that her angry outburst had to do with Maria. She stood before her aunt, arms hanging, somewhat pale but quite composed. Her face was dead straight. I even had the impression she was stifling a laugh.

"When with one last loud outburst the aunt finally stopped shouting and slammed her door behind her, Maria Luisa said to me: 'Ernesto, you'll help me prepare dinner, won't you, and wash the few dishes afterwards? You see,' she added, squinting slyly at the crack in the door to her aunt's room, 'she's thrown out our Odilia.'

"When we were alone in the kitchen she told me a few details, but only in fits and starts. I took her hesitancy for a reluctance to be open with me. It troubled me. Much later on, in Germany, when I thought about how Maria Luisa would pick up on one thing or another, I often thought of the incident with Odilia and I always came to the conclusion: her sense of justice, of right and wrong was already strong then.

"So, the aunt dismissed Odilia because she was secretly sharing her room with a stranger. It emerged that none of us knew the young woman, Theodosio's sister or cousin, as Maria later revealed. Allegedly she was looking for work and her family lived far away in the favelas. She always left the house before daybreak. Odilia often brought her a hot coffee or a little bread or a banana.

"Odilia lived in a wretched room stored with any amount of old junk. I couldn't for the life of me see how Theodosio's sister ever found any space in a hole like that.

"Neighbors coming home from a party saw a stranger slipping out of this room and asked the aunt if she was aware that her maid was sheltering an unknown woman.

"At the time, it was strictly forbidden to have unregistered strangers stay overnight. There were often raids. You could be severely punished. Luckily—for the stranger, I mean—the aunt couldn't hold her tongue and wait until that night to make sure for herself. There and then she confronted Odilia with renewed rage. Odilia wasn't clever enough to argue. Her bundle was tiny. Within ten minutes she had vanished into the city, after once more looking in at Theodosio's booth. This unknown woman never came back either.

"To all our surprise the very next day an old man, small and shrunken, skin neither black nor brown (just dust caught in the folds), had taken over the repair booth. Aunt Elfriede failed to see any connection. I was too proud to ask Maria. She was clearly in the picture.

"Shortly before I left, or was it on our trip to Belo Horizonte, in any case suddenly Maria Luisa felt she needed to reveal everything to me, every last thing, not to be left behind with any secrets kept hidden, as though even the slightest secret could jeopardize our being together again. Unasked, she told me what happened that time with Odilia and Theodosio and the unknown girl. The girl wasn't related to the cobbler at all. He had merely been given the job of arranging somewhere for her to stay in Rio. Even now Maria didn't reveal where and by whom, or else she didn't know. The stranger was followed all the way from Recife; the police were on her trail from the start. But at the same time her party here had tipped her off: police were waiting for her at the train station in Rio. But she had already left the train hours, if not days, before and changed from one bus to the next until finally arriving in Rio without incident. The first thing she did then was look up the man whose address she had carefully kept with her: Theodosio.

"Theodosio quickly took her to Odilia. They had made this arrangement long ago; they had been expecting the girl from Recife. Odilia, who had good sense as well as a simple nature, took in the stranger at once. She would probably have fed and sheltered her for many more weeks had these damnable neighbors who stuck their noses into everything not interfered.

"The girl from Recife made a swift getaway (of course, by now the police had lost the scent). Maybe she really did have friends or relatives in the favelas. Poor Odilia had no decent alternative accommodation. She only had those people at the market who offered her a pretty miserable existence. But she had heart and sense enough to warn Theodosio of the danger that threatened him too, so that he disappeared immediately after Odilia's report.

"'We had all gained Brazilian citizenship long ago,' Maria said. 'For you, as foreigners, to not register or to know anything about Odilia would have been particularly risky. And you might not have kept your mouth shut, Ernesto, and perhaps said something to your father.'

"I saw Odilia again by chance at a market. She was selling fruit. Probably she slept under the fruit cart at night like before. She didn't recognize me and I didn't want to speak to her either.

"I tell you this incident because it sheds light on the way the girl acted, how Maria Luisa thought—what she was like then in our luminous youth. Later, when I was in Germany and her letters suddenly became dismissive and unintelligible, I always thought: *what shone like that can't just suddenly be extinguished*.

"Shortly after getting rid of Odilia, Aunt Elfriede took on a white girl, a German one in fact. Her name was Emma. She was from somewhere in the state of Santa Catarina. The place (a large village or small provincial town) was in the middle of a German colony. The Brazilians who lived among them or had land nearby both respected and despised the German colonists. They respected them for their tireless diligence and their integrity. They despised them for almost the same reasons, because they made rapid, almost merciless progress with their livestock, their fields and their businesses, and because it was always done honestly. However, the locals thought it couldn't go on honestly forever.

"Aunt Elfriede's new housemaid was certainly thoroughly honest. The moment we set eyes on her we children couldn't stand her. But strangely, she didn't even notice, in fact she was devoted to us. She also remained with Maria Luisa afterwards. I tell you so much about Emma because she has a certain role to play later.

"Aunt Elfriede almost got rid of her again right away when she heard the requested salary. 'I can never, ever pay that much,' she exclaimed. But Emma—who had already ascertained that Aunt Elfriede ran a small business and finished blouses and dresses in the evening hours—quickly responded: 'I have always wanted to work for a real German family. But I cannot possibly accept the position for less. How about if I was to take the needlework off your hands? I never go out in the evening anyway; I leave that to the mulatto girls.'

"Aunt Elfriede considered the offer and eventually concluded it could be to her advantage, as later proved the case: suddenly she had far more free time; the half-finished garments were stitched together to a very high standard, exactly according to the patterns (though we still saw Emma in the same old dull dresses and blouses).

"After some to-and-fro, the only outstanding grievance was the abysmal room in the filthy, cluttered attic. Odilia was ascribed the blame. And Emma from Santa Catarina immediately set to tidying it. She piled up the unsightly clutter and covered it with a washed curtain. After fumigating the bed, she covered it with another curtain. She painted the walls golden yellow and hung up all kinds of pictures: an image of Christ (the people in Santa Catarina were evangelical), a calendar, and some photographs of her relatives (though to my knowledge they never got in touch).

"Although Aunt Elfriede never really took a liking to her, Emma soon became indispensable; she was used for all sorts of secret jobs and errands—you'll hear more about that later."

All at once Triebel's expression changed. He looked pleased, almost happy. He gestured towards the sea. "There! Look, there!"

At first I thought sea spray to sparkle in the sun. Then I made out one or two fish flying over the water, seeming to dance over the sea's surface, then whole shoals gliding in and out of each other in the sunlight, as Triebel gave me a running commentary with a contented look on his face as I hadn't seen before.

Because we were in the shade and could see everything from where we stood, the Polish children came over to us. Unlike me, this wasn't the first time they had seen flying fish, having made the journey various times before, but they too were captivated.

By the time afternoon settled over the ocean, the fish had flown off. They regularly returned while we sailed in the south and like the children and like Triebel, I took pleasure in their flight. I don't know why they made me feel uplifted.

I had begun this long sea journey almost with reluctance, without imagining what new things I might get to see. Until now I thought such pleasures only existed on dry land, for instance on seeing the countryside, meadows and trees.

Now thoughtful, now irrepressibly happy, interrupting himself again and again to point out a single flying fish or an entire shoal, Triebel carried on: "By this time we were practically grown up. We often lay nestled together on the beach in a dip in the sand or a gap in the rocks, simply expressing our belonging together, as though there was nothing remarkable to it, nor anything suggestive or physical. We casually watched the other young couples, mainly black or mulatto, happily and harmlessly play out their love scenes unconcerned, perhaps in the next sand dune or elsewhere nearby.

"That sort of thing didn't interest us. Not at all? Not in the slightest? We gave it no thought. Sometimes Maria Luisa ran her mouth over my temples and looked at me expectantly but I jumped up and ran away like a boy, and she ran after me. We threw ourselves onto the sand and I wrapped my arms around her head. It was always only ever about how much we belonged together, nothing wild or unrestrained.

"That's how it felt to me, later on too, for the rest of our childhood. Whether Maria Luisa saw it exactly the same I cannot say for sure.

"We both passed our final exams together. On my father's advice and also of my own accord I began my medical studies. Maria Luisa likewise asked him for advice because she had no one she could confide in. We somehow saw our future plans interwoven, just as our childhoods had seemed interwoven until now. My father advised Maria Luisa to specialize in either pediatrics or child psychology, should she feel greater affinity for either. He spoke seriously and thoroughly with her.

"Her aunt would have been happy to have her serve in her shop from that moment forth and attract as many customers as possible. Laughing, Maria Luisa told me Aunt Elfriede was forever saying to her that a girl her age here gets married: 'Have you no serious suitors? This Triebel, he's not earnest.'

"Maria Luisa had a small inheritance from her father that would just about cover her studies and this sustained her for the time being.

"The Second World War was drawing to a close, and sometimes when we were alone my father said: 'I'll write to my friend, Paul Winter, or Professor Buschmann, so I get a place to go right away and can start with work, because there's no doubt they'll need me, badly need me.'

"At the time, I didn't give what he said much thought. The war was far away. Its destructive fire was far away. Only now and then did we breathe the smoke.

"For the smoke, it reached us. We saw harrowing things in the newspapers and the cinemas. We couldn't believe that our gentle and quiet native land should suddenly have pierced the world like a thorn.

"'Can it really be true?' Maria Luisa asked me. She held my hand anxiously. It was around the time that the Soviets discovered the first extermination camps. 'I was still a very small child,' she said, 'so only now do I remember our washerwoman. How kind she was! I loved it when my mother let me take her something. There were flowers on her windowsill, summer and winter. And the nun who nursed my mother until her death, not only did she look like Mary from those engravings of the *Visitation of Mary* or the *Annunciation*, she also had the corresponding heart, prepared for everything. I've never told you much about that time, Ernst, but today as we see together the horrors that German people seem to have committed, I see myself in strange contrast inside the washerwoman's flower-darkened room once more, and I hear the nun's voice, not so much deathly sad as deathly glad.'

"She came home with me to pour out her heart to my father.

"'Do you think the entire population here had a part in the evils that Vargas or a squad of his soldiers committed? Or rampaging landowners?' he said to her.

"Once Maria Luisa had gone home, I said to my father, 'You're right in what you say. I just don't follow this idea you have to go back to a country rotting away like that.'

"'That is exactly where we're urgently needed. You'll see it yourself.'

"However, the war was still far from over then. Thoughts of leaving were rarely expressed aloud.

"Our classmate Eliza had started her studies at a music academy. She often played for us, but not only that, she also showed us books and pictures that we might never have set eyes on but for her.

"We were moved, Maria Luisa and I, enthralled even, when we saw the work of Aleijadinho for the very first time: the prophets Isaiah, Jeremiah, Ezekiel and others, which he sculpted on a flight of stairs in Congonhas do Campo. This stairway was a Passion Path from the valley to the church built high above. Eliza told us that, not only was Aleijadinho the greatest artist in the country, maybe one of the greatest artists there had ever been, he had been a leper. He sculpted everything from his thoughts without hands, with arm stumps gradually melting away like candles, and his little helper strapped pins to his stumps.

"Eliza was right. There can be nothing greater on earth. That's what we children thought at the time, comparing him with paintings from the antiquity and the Renaissance and all that we discovered through Eliza in terms of great works of art we had never seen before.

"I say so much about this artist here on the ship because the trip to Congonhas was probably our last magical-marvelous experience together in that country.

"You see, because we kept on at my father about Aleijadinho in great excitement—as though, rather than study photographs of his work, we had out of the blue met the dying but mighty man himself—suddenly he had the idea to give us the present of a trip to Minas Gerais. That's the name of the state Congonhas is in.

"'Don't you want to see all these wonderful things yourself?' I asked him.

"But he shook his head: 'No, children. You should enjoy yourselves.'

"I think now that the war must already have ended; our journey back home must already have been confirmed. Perhaps even so it was actually only certain in his mind and I still didn't believe it would happen, so that he could just as easily have said: you should enjoy yourselves together one more time.

"I'm also not entirely sure what made him think to suddenly send two young people who loved each other far away.

"Of course, by today's standards it wasn't all that far away: a twelve hour bus journey to Belo Horizonte. That's the name of the main city in Minas Gerais; Congonhas do Campo is nearby.

"Maria explained to me that a lot of gold was mined there at the time of the Portuguese viceroys and during the emperor's reign.

"Nestled together, we set off with our little food parcels into the strange allure of the far unknown. As though it had wings, the bus was soon swinging round the edge of vertiginous, heart-stoppingly steep precipices.

"Excuse me telling you so much about the region, but soon you'll see the most important thing recur; yes, so that by recurring in our lives it becomes something significant and doesn't sink into unfathomable mystery."

"No!" I cried. "Quite the opposite, Triebel; please tell me all about your trip."

Strictly speaking, I preferred Triebel to describe the landscape, what he had seen of it, rather than go on about his love life. I also couldn't quite work out why he was telling *me* so much about his life. Why not Günter Bartsch, for instance, with whom he seemed to have made friends a little? Perhaps because I was silent through all that he said, and asked no questions and voiced no opinion—because I had none. Perhaps that was why he told everything to me, the silent man; the man with no opinion.

"So we crossed over Minas Gerais state border. At our first short stop, wretched-looking traders crowded round the bus with little polished pebbles and fragments of cobalt and agate and all sorts of semi-precious stones. Obviously it wasn't hard to find them here. The road seemed to sparkle with them; in some places it seemed thickly strewn with shards of semi-precious stones.

"Either side of the road we saw things we'd never set eyes on before. We were shocked and at the same time filled with burning curiosity. Our fellow passengers explained to us that the pointed, regular hillocks that looked as though an architect had designed them were termite mounds and that, when the termites left for whatever reason, snakes moved into their empty homes.

"The streets, the trees, the huts were gradually being covered in a reddish, ferrous sulphur dust. Even the few garments of washing in the yard of one hut were dusted red, as was the meager lone banana tree that fed the occupants.

"At some stops the passengers got out to eat and drink. The two of us, we watched what we spent. We just bought something from the children who came racing up to us with all kinds of fruit, black and white children all in rags. Their pieces of fruit had been prepared with great care, perhaps the night before, as though they too were precious stones. They offered us oranges (the two halves sliced up) as well as pineapple and sugar cane.

"Eliza had found us somewhere to stay with relatives in Belo Horizonte. We were given a friendly welcome, but without a great song and dance. It was a warm night. We slept on the veranda. Early in the morning we drank hot coffee nearby and ventured into this new unfamiliar mountain region. The villages glistened in the dawn. The forest smelt good.

"'Perhaps Thuringia looks similar, or the Harz,' I said.

"'Ah, no, I think everything looks very different there,' Maria replied.

"Now I saw the wild, untamed forest through her eyes, as

well as the collapsing verandas in front of the huts—no one in these families had strength enough left to prop them back up.

"Because our bus stopped in Congonhas, we didn't arrive in the valley like the pilgrims; we had to walk down to the church from where we got off in the village above. We had already spotted it at a distance, above rooftops and trees, shimmering white in the morning light. We made for it swiftly and silently.

"Eager with anticipation, rather than go inside we went straight down the grand sweeping stairway.

"We stopped directly in front of the first plinth and looked up in awe at the folds in the prophet's robe. What we saw for the first time in its beauty and majesty almost struck fear into us. Maria Luisa gently placed her hand on the stone. Slowly she traced one of the carved folds.

"Suddenly a monk stood between us. He had come out of the church and watched on in silence. Now he offered to tell us one or two things. Firstly he took us back into the church. Maria Luisa crossed herself. She never went to church at home and I had never asked her if she had been baptized a Catholic.

"As we stepped back from the prophets, the monk said: 'Look here; his apprentice strapped a chisel to his arm stump. You see it in the grooves that form the folds. But the face looks as though the artist needed no hands, only thoughts.'

"The monk accompanied us, one flight of stairs after another, prophet after prophet. We exchanged a few words here and there, Maria and I, whereupon the monk asked us in German: 'Hey, children, where are you from?'

"'From Thuringia,' we told him. 'I'm from Ilmenau.'—'I'm from Erfurt.'

"And he said: 'I come from Bavaria.' He told us that his order had sent him here several years ago.

"'Do you not get homesick?' I said.

"'For where? My home is always with me,' he replied, smiling.

"'I mean your real home.'

"'Ah, children, are we going to argue about where's really home?'

"He asked us nothing more. He came down to the bottom of the valley with us. As we said goodbye he mentioned in a friendly way: 'If you want to stay somewhere reasonable you could go to our hospice, up there on the right.'

"But we had already agreed to go back to Belo Horizonte later that evening.

"He left us in front of the grotto in the valley. He wished us a safe journey home.

"We decided to slowly climb back up, as though on a pilgrimage. We overtook an old mulatto lady in a crumpled dress brought along on the journey. You saw how hard she found the climb.

"'What is she murmuring away to herself?' I asked Maria Luisa.

"Maria Luisa, who was nimbly pulling me along, said half-seriously, half in the tone of a poem: 'Hail, Maria, full of grace. May the Lord be with you. Blessed art thou among women, and blessed is the fruit of thy womb, Jesus. Amen. Holy Maria, mother of God, intercede for us poor sinners now and in the hour of our death.'

"'What sense is there in repeating these same words over

and over?' I said to her.

"For a moment I thought she hadn't heard me, when suddenly she said, 'No, it has sense. You too have the same thoughts constantly, the same wish. It's contained in the words.'

"A year later, before we parted she said to me: 'You remember our trip to Congonhas do Campo? When I was there on the steps I prayed and prayed for you to stay. I'm probably not strong enough; I'm probably not good enough, so that no one heard me.'

"We cried, and I patted her and swore she was the best of all.

"Fleetingly I wondered why she had given me this heavy burden on my journey, and almost immediately (or a second later) I asked myself: *why did I think such a thing?*"

Suddenly Günther Bartsch stepped between us, the fresh-faced, bright young man who ate at Triebel's table. "Let's meet on the bridge tonight, Triebel, like yesterday. And you, Hammer," he said, turning to me, "I suggest you come up with us if you really want to get a good look at the Southern Cross on this journey before it slips out of the southern night sky."

I agreed at once. I looked forward to my astronomy lesson.

That afternoon, Triebel asked me to accompany him. I knew he was happiest talking about important things while walking. "My father", he began, "probably received the decisive letter in the spring of '46, from Germany, from his old work colleague who had already written to him two or three times since the end of the war. My father firstly read the letter himself, with great anticipation and attention. Then he read it aloud. The letter said that the universities in Germany would reopen. There was still a desperate shortage in all professions and those who realized this were set to teach and study because the war-torn people in the ruined cities needed both as much as bread; however, the rebuilding plans were already in place.

"My father was not slow to speak for himself: a doctor of his specialism and attitude was desperately needed, he said. He didn't yet know in which city he would be placed. With regards to me, wishing to apply myself to internal medicine, he said I would need to complete my studies in Berlin or another city.

"I refused categorically. I told him that on no account did I wish to part from Maria Luisa; and all the reasons my father proposed for returning to Germany as swiftly as possible made no impact on me.

"My father listened in silence and then responded: 'Maria Luisa. Well, if she can't raise the money to come with us now, no doubt there you can soon earn money for her journey. She probably still has a little herself.'

"For all my frantic opposition, my father made clear to me in no uncertain terms that I would never manage to train as a doctor on my own here. How would I feed myself? Fund my studies? My upkeep? Accommodation? Perhaps I would want to take up another career for Maria's sake? A salesman in some shop? Then that's me be busy into the night. And anything else would only be harder, he said. I would go to ruin. His friends had only sent him money for our journey back. He couldn't leave me any behind.

"I would have to knock my studies on the head, he said, because as I well knew, any training was expensive, so if I wanted to stand on my own two feet I would have to find a job or learn a trade.

"In Germany—in the east of Germany, that is—I could sensibly finish my studies and then be useful to lots of people, and that was what mattered, he said; and what's more, if I didn't want to leave her, Maria Luisa could come over after a certain time.

"This wasn't our only conversation. We talked often, back and forth. My father, who until then I had only known as my friend, was adamant about the matter. He was the stronger of us both. I won't dwell on all the ins and outs.

"'I knew you were going to go,' Maria Luisa said to me.

"But what with preparations for the journey and waiting for our passports, some time passed. During these weeks, as though by agreement, suddenly we no longer spoke of farewells. We lay nestled together on the beach. Only once did I sense her face was wet with tears.

"'Rest assured the money for your crossing will soon be here too,' I said to her, adding, 'if your aunt or Eliza won't lend you enough.'

"'Ah, my Aunt Elfriede,' Maria said gloomily, 'what she says or thinks is as colored as her hair.' She sat up and said angrily: 'She always wanted to make me work in her clothes shop. She would demand exactly the same of you.'

"From day one I wrote to Maria Luisa about everything I saw in Germany.

"Millions of war dead. Millions, millions. But what I saw—what was it the punishment for? Cities in ruins, hollow-eyed people who, insofar as they had strength left to walk, dragged themselves to a distribution point to be given little bags full of oats or barley and their bread ration or a handful of sugar. And in Berlin too, searching for my father's friends we clambered over mountains of rubble, through streets that no longer existed. The young and the old rooted through rubble for anything they could use or sell, be it a solitary screw or the remains of a mattress. We saw right through collapsed houses into bedrooms and bathrooms. Sometimes someone emerged from inside. Once, everything collapsed in front of our eyes and the occupants were buried in the rubble.

"Before that, in Antwerp, where our ship briefly docked, it had felt very strange indeed to hear an animated discussion about whether fish offal (soft and hard roe) should be sent to the hungry children in devastated Germany.

"Such was the hatred in the stricken countries towards Nazi soldiers, who had killed so many people and destroyed villages and towns, that it affected even the children.

"I might have been better not to mention such experiences and conversations in my letters to Maria Luisa…"

He broke off from his account. He was silent.

"No," I said. "There's no easy answer to that. For years you were used to speaking openly with your girl about everything. And aside from you two, what went on during this war will long remain a conundrum for many people, a terrible conundrum.

But those who aren't inured must try to solve the conundrum."

"What kind of a conundrum?"

"Well, the inhumanity, the cruelty of a nation that gave birth to Goethe, Beethoven, and I don't know who all else."

"Did everyone suddenly turn cruel and inhuman? I'm not sure. I tried to compare everything I saw before me on my way through the shattered city with something I knew. I thought of the long journey Maria Luisa and I made by bus to Minas Gerais, dilapidated huts caked in red dust. Life in these huts had seemed intolerable to us then, but now it seemed intolerable to live in one of these ruins, in a corner open to the wind.

"The first room I stayed in was in pretty good condition, despite the glued-together window panes. My landlady was an old woman. She told me where and when, on which part of the continent she lost each of her sons, grandchildren and brothers. She wasn't actually angry; all the houses to the front had been obliterated, meaning that after having gazed into a dingy yard her whole life, she now looked onto a wide street with trees.

"Sometimes two or three little old ladies came to visit, to behold me, the stranger; above all, because my old landlady gave them Brazilian coffee beans. They counted them out literally hours on end to ensure each got her rightful amount.

"Soon a terrible thing happened in this house which even shocked my hardened landlady. Below us lived a family with the grandfather and several children. As happened virtually everywhere, the mother of the family marked the bread portions out beforehand. Frantic from hunger, during the night the grandfather sneaked into the kitchen, bit into the loaf and devoured a piece several portions wide. The oldest boy woke up and caught him unawares, and from fear and shame the grandfather stabbed the boy at will with the breadknife.

"I wrote about this incident too, like I did about everything I experienced, in a long letter to Maria. In so doing I didn't appreciate that she couldn't possibly make head or tail of these diary-like letters. The postal service was in disarray. Maria Luisa was far away on another continent. When I got her first letter, though not used to my surroundings, by then they had lost their terrible impact. I wondered whether I should specialize in pediatrics or tropical medicine. I sensed there was a desperate need for pediatricians. An institute for tropical medicine was still unthinkable then.

"Maria Luisa wrote to me at the house where the old man killed his grandson. She said that she couldn't imagine remaining proud and considerate in such an environment, and that for her was the prerequisite for an honest life. She did admire me, but would our love not suffer if continually exposed to such insensitivity, such hardship? But I would write to her about everything, *everything*, so she might feel she was with me, might feel me near a little.

"Yes, people were hungry and wicked... I must tell you everything, even though you know about it. Otherwise you wouldn't understand the special situation that arose for Maria and me. Because this special thing (as I've called it several times already) only found its end a short time ago, on the evening before our departure. How long have we been underway now?"

"Wait a moment. Five days, I think."

"Then it ended conclusively six days ago. If such a thing really exists: reaching a conclusion, finding an end. Where was

I?"

"How wicked and hungry people were."

"In the unlit trams that crossed the city all you heard were desperate reports, angry outbursts, appeals for help. I can remember one day in one such crowded tram, or was it at a station, a strange sound took everyone by surprise: a rousing chorus, sung with drive and gusto. People pricked up their ears, they shook their heads. It was a few more stations before their cursing and complaining began again.

"A little later, I learned that a group of the newly-formed Free German Youth (*Freie Deutsche Jugend*, FJD) had sung the song.

"When I became a student soon after that, the FDJ were starting to form at the universities too. Many who joined were genuinely anti-fascist, hated the old and felt in accord with the Soviet occupation and the new laws. At the time FDJ members weren't exclusively treated like prodigal sons (brothers and fathers had been, perhaps remained, Nazi); sometimes they were attacked on the street, even badly beaten up.

"I joined a group that formed in my medical faculty.

"Luckily for me, around that time a kind of temporary student housing was set up. Generally there were three or four to a room. But as I told you, I wasn't used to a big apartment. I made my suitcase into a desk like during our exile. Our professors were a real mix: excellent doctors who are now almost famous, but also a few charlatans teaching under false pretences. And this soon came to light and they were hounded out. Many students half-way through their courses studied diligently in our midst.

"Once, during the Nuremberg Trials (which were still running then), a young doctor was cited. He had administered lethal injections to dozens of prisoners as an intern at a concentration camp. He was never prosecuted. He had shot himself.

"We students talked about this incident late into the night. In those days, everyone plainly spoke their mind. Some, but not many, openly expressed sympathy with the dead man. Others stressed his guilt. There were also some who indignantly declared that it was a disgrace to punish people who had observed their duty of obedience during the war. Such views were voiced by many older students who had suspended their studies during the war, perhaps previously followers of Hitler.

"There was a hopeless jumble of opinions. Sympathy? How so? Why a duty of obedience? What do the Nuremberg Trials have to do with it?

"All at once a very young female student spoke. She didn't stand out; she was neither attractive nor talkative. 'If a wrong has taken place,' she said, 'and who can doubt that in this case, then there is also a trial. Whether atonement comes through the so-called Nuremberg Trials or by shooting oneself dead as this unfortunate man has done, there can be no doubt as to his guilt.'

"Until then, no one in our group had noticed this girl. Suddenly it was deathly quiet. We had listened so intently, now we were thinking it over. All at once I had the sensation that Maria Luisa had appeared in our midst; this girl had stated her opinion in a soft but decisive voice. I felt more homesick than ever in recent days. I was convinced a letter would arrive tomorrow.

"I would like to reiterate that everyone in our circle candidly expressed their views. At the time, everyone still decided right from wrong according to their own discretion. The pale quiet girl had expressed her view clearest of all.

"Afterwards I happened to notice a young man called Gustav (who later became the leader of our FDJ group) sit down beside the girl and say to her: 'I agree with you: a man like that should be put on trial and severely punished.'

"And you see, Hammer, I made the mistake of writing to my Maria Luisa about every discussion, every incident, as in a diary. But how could she have sympathized, understood anything? My letters could only have driven her to despair, nothing less. And when it was too late I discovered that my letters had affected her in this way. I, though, I kept waiting for a reply, one that would give me comfort and strength. But when a letter came it said: 'I couldn't stand a life like yours.'

"But there were good things too," Triebel continued. "And had Maria remained the person she was in our youth then she would have read such a letter about such an incident with amazement.

"One day Gustav took me along to some factory. A Soviet lieutenant was giving a talk. In particular he was willing to answer questions. The place was pretty packed. It was stuffy and smoky, but chilly even so. The lieutenant was perhaps only three years older than me. At first people asked miscellaneous questions about work, wages and schools in the Soviet Union. Suddenly a young man stood up, probably as old as the lieutenant. His colleagues must have sensed something insolent was set to issue forth from his sneering mouth because a silence descended; a provocative silence. Most were already smiling as he shouted in a sharp voice: 'Herr Lieutenant, I too would like to ask you something.'

"'Yes, please?'

"'You stole my pocket watch. When will you give it back?'

"Everyone was silent, highly amused and highly attentive.

"'Are you making a demand of me, then?' this extremely young lieutenant calmly said.

"'Indeed I am,' the young man replied, if possible even more brazenly, even more bluntly. The entire room held its collective breath in veiled amusement, awaiting the response.

"'I come from the Ukraine,' the lieutenant said. 'You probably know that the Ukraine is the richest corn-growing country in Europe. Despite that, my father starved to death there during the occupation. My mother died when they burnt down half the village. My sister was taken into forced labor in Germany. I have heard nothing of her since. My older brother was killed in the war. My younger died in a prison camp. Now let me come back to your demand. I demand my father and my mother, my sister and my two brothers. You demand your pocket watch. Do you uphold your demand?'

"The young worker said nothing. I think he swiftly and silently left the hall.

"It had grown quiet around us. Though further questions were put, it was primarily by older people or others asking seriously, exercising restraint. Everyone was regarding the lieutenant with awe, with something like reverence.

"I wrote to Maria Luisa about this incident too, but you see, three months went by before I received a reply. It was quite brief. The entire letter was about other matters.

"Meanwhile, I had got to know a publisher who published French, Spanish and Portuguese authors. During our conversations I suggested to him the novel *The Mulatto*. He took me up on it and was happy with my sample translation, and I with his offer. *Now I can put away money more quickly for Maria Luisa's journey here*, I thought.

"When I finally heard from her (in response to me telling her about the money for her fare and the incident with the Soviet lieutenant), the letter seemed strangely incoherent, as though three people had written it in confusion. But all the same it came from there and the writing was all but her image. I also felt a softer tone emanate: my life was hard enough; I mustn't make myself ill toiling away on her account; if I fell seriously ill, what would that achieve?

"I reassured her that I was well, that I felt strong.

"I was preparing for an exam. At the same time I was getting used to translating long into the night."

That night, I climbed up onto the bridge as arranged. Bartsch and Triebel would be along soon. Though I grew up in the countryside and had often spent the night out-of-doors, it struck me that I had never seen stars so bright. We probably didn't even have stars as bright as those above me in the southern sky. When I looked long enough a shimmering spiral showed in the blue-black sky, completely unimpeded either by a town periphery, tower or mountains. But the shimmering spiral was stronger still in its reflection on the sea, calm yet perpetually moving of its own accord. I no longer understood why, rather than stand here, I had spent several nights trying to sleep, or calming down a drunken Woytek, or chatting with Sadowski, or playing chess with the Polish boy, or smoking, or whatever else.

Triebel and Bartsch came up.

Bartsch took pains with me so that I located the Southern Cross, which had moved into the southwest along with the entire constellation of Sagittarius, which it followed.

I was amazed how well Triebel knew this sky. He, so utterly bewildered by events concerning him here below, seemed to have a crystal-clear understanding when he identified something in the night sky.

"I previously imagined the Southern Cross as something huge," he said, "so I was disappointed when a teacher pointed it out to me. These stars which connected create a cross must have been something enthralling, unparalleled for all the conquerors, the symbol of conquest standing before them by which they set their ships' course."

"Oh, yes," Bartsch said, "it became a symbol for them, an orientation for their ships and captains, and in their imaginations it probably shone down from heaven. And it still has this imaginary luster for us today."

"It's already slipped," Triebel said. "Soon it will leave our field of vision. But when we are home again in the north I will long for these stars."

"Why?" I said. "Our sky is strewn with stars too if we really look up."

"But I will long for these in particular."

Bartsch patiently outlined to me the course from star to star that finally led to the Great Bear.

Triebel resumed his train of thought: "If we imagine conquistadors set out from the south and advanced into the north, then they could only have grasped the magnitude of the universe from the stars; because they would have traveled by ship from south to north. Eventually they would leave the Southern Cross behind, which until then they had held as sacred. After crossing the equator the Pole Star would arise before them and the constellation that we call the Little Bear. The Pole Star would probably have become the guiding star and enduring symbol for these conquistadors. Of course, these conquerors from the south are entirely my own making."

Bartsch replied to my question by saying he came from Silesia. His father had been a professor in industry there. He himself studied at the Mining Academy in Freiberg. Perhaps he paid so much attention to stars because his job concerned the inside of mountains.

*N*ext morning, Triebel caught me by the arm and pulled me to our usual place. He spoke at me hurriedly and frenetically, as though he could alter the events he was heading towards.

"Gustav, the leader of my group, might have become my friend, could I have brought myself to trust anyone back then. But I was completely and utterly consumed by love. Sometimes

I ran to the other side of the street in the feeling that Maria Luisa had just turned the corner. Every day I waited on tenterhooks for news. And when none came, which was mostly the case, I was wracked by torment.

"But I hardly had a spare minute—fortunately, I can say now. We had to work a lot; I had an interim assessment looming. In addition there was the separate work I had obtained from the publisher.

"One day, when I happened to be sitting alone somewhere, thinking over a turn of phrase in Maria Luisa's last letter, a phrase that seemed unclear and ambiguous, as though by chance Gustav sat down beside me. He said in a not unfriendly way that he wanted to discuss something urgent. I broke off from my train of thought as one slams shut a book.

"'Say, Ernst,' he began, 'you're fairly well on with your studies now. You're making progress. Why do you participate so little in our life? Only rarely do you come to one of our meetings of an evening. You never go to the lectures. You always live alone.'

"'Aside from the interim assessment I have looming, I have a deadline on some work for a publisher. There's no one apart from me who translates from the Portuguese,' I replied haltingly.

"Gustav thought for a moment. That too was why I had time for him, because he thought about people and never gave a stock answer. 'I can understand that you're still attached to that country, its language, its books and its people,' he said eventually. 'But don't you think it's time you really got to know the country that is your own at the end of the day? It strikes me as more important that you argue with our students and put forward our opinion than you spend half the night translating for this publisher.'

"'I've signed a contract,' I said, somewhat curtly. 'The translation's urgent.'

"But now Gustav didn't hold back. 'Your father,' he replied, 'has a professorship in Greifswald. He sends you what you need. You said so once yourself. You have your scholarship. Why struggle away with this difficult publishing work? You're not obliged to earn money, are you?'

"I immediately regretted my response: 'No, no, I am; I don't need the money myself, but a person close to me needs it as swiftly as possible.'

"Gustav said nothing. However, he looked so taken aback that I told him the all-important thing: 'As you know, we lived in Brazil for many years. I was and still am attached to a girl there. You can't imagine a closer friendship. We want to be together again as swiftly as possible. But the journey's expensive. So I have to push myself, to save for her fare.'

"'But you can't, Ernst, when you actually think about it. If the girl really wants to come here to be with you, then you'll have to think of something else. You're not making headway with this struggling and saving.'

"I wanted to answer back but swallowed my reply. He let me be. I think, though, that he kept on thinking about me. I think he was far too straightforward, too unused to difficulties like those pertaining to my plan. Or perhaps he actually had thought of them and didn't want to say anything.

"I myself almost despaired during those days because I had finally worked out for myself (as Gustav had probably quickly worked out) that Maria Luisa would only use a fraction of the considerable sum I was acquiring. I chose to delay the transfer until I had the payment in my hands after delivering the completed translation. I wrote to Maria Luisa that now she only need wait three more months and then her fare would be all but secure; I thought it better to send everything at once rather than in installments.

"It wasn't long before I received a reply. I opened the letter hurriedly but carefully, so that it didn't tear, as though I could thereby hurt Maria. But when I read it I stopped short. I read the letter over and over, and once I knew certain phrases by heart, I started to ruminate. Maria Luisa had sometimes used a strange turn of phrase before, leading me to believe she was beginning to have doubts about our seeing each other again. What it said in this letter was: 'My dear Ernst, please don't send me money for my fare. If I was suddenly to come, I could probably obtain the necessary money here somehow. But don't you keep saving for me; clearly it means a grueling amount of work for you. I don't want the money and I don't need it.'

"My first thought was she had abandoned the idea of coming to me, and my heart turned heavy as lead. Then I thought again: *she's thinking the same as Gustav*. But during dark nights of deep despair I sensed her will for a shared existence weakening, had she not lost the desire altogether. I lay awake in the night tormenting myself and suddenly I thought: *you can live unhappily too. Who among all the raucous, cat-calling night owls has really found what they long for? I have my studies that I'm committed to; I have friends like Gustav*. I decided to go and see him and with his help set my whole life straight. Because he was right—this constant waiting was wearing me out.

"I wrote to Maria Luisa that her last letter had been incomprehensible; she must let me know if I could send the money to her old address. To this she again urgently pleaded with me not to send her money under any circumstances: 'You're not trying to cause me grief, are you?' is what she wrote. But she also wrote: 'Can you imagine what my aunt would do if she got hold of the money? In fact it's probably better you send your letters to Eliza.' And she added (as though it had the remotest bearing on us): 'Since you've been gone my friend Eliza has become a major artist. When she plays she can move you to happiness or despair.'

"Though this Eliza was of no concern to me, I suddenly saw her before me: an unappealing bony girl, taciturn with almond eyes. But when she sat at the piano—all at once you were in another world.

"I wrote back, but only after a certain time, so Maria too might learn what waiting meant: it had become clear to me that time had a hold over her; that all her promises had vanished like air, otherwise she would use any means necessary to be united with me.

"Of course, I didn't mention the money the publisher had paid me. I didn't actually believe what I wrote to Maria. My heart surged with joy when she wrote back after a certain interval (but not overly long), asking how I could even think such a thing regarding the irrevocable promises of our youth.

"She used the word 'youth' as though we had aged during our separation. I really was shocked when I calculated the time (being honest with myself for perhaps the first time since we parted) because in fact days, months, even years had passed…

"Around that time, there were far more debating nights with the students. They were genuine debates. No one kept their views hidden. The chair for the evening stuck to some theme, for instance a new book, and encouraged questions. Then you often heard opinions that were crass and erroneous, but open and honest whereas now, relatively few years later, most young people only say what is accepted as right. They certainly don't lie, but they don't wrestle with doubt or dissent. They await the accepted view. Then they firmly believe it, and there's the rub, because then they themselves accept it from the outset."

"We had nothing like that," I said. "There can be no doubt about a repair, because it's immediately obvious who was right. Or awaiting what was accepted in a construction—you can't, for the same reason."

"Wait, though; I cannot believe you never encountered such sentiments. You just never spoke about them.

"One well-attended evening in the assembly hall, Gustav was chairing and beside him sat a Soviet cultural officer, not much older than him. One of the first to ask to speak was a student whom I only knew by sight. He had a prosthetic limb in place of his left arm. He spoke highly articulately, easily audible throughout the hall: 'I too read the book of which you speak. It did not appeal to me and I cannot agree with the praise you afford it. To my mind it is a saccharine book, mendacious even. It would have me feel certain things. However, to be frank, I am suspicious of all feelings. After my experiences in the war and under Nazism, I have made one firm resolve: never again to be taken in by a feeling; I only trust opinions born of the intellect, which the intellect proves to me in black and white. All else is superfluous.'

"A short, somewhat stunned silence followed. Then the officer suddenly said: 'What you have just said is also a feeling. But I can explain it to you with my intellect. Where do we draw the line?'

"He probably had more to add, but I stood up. 'If you love a girl,' I said, 'what has that to do with your intellect? With proof?'

"I realized Gustav knew to what I alluded, but I no longer cared. No one smiled, rather they listened in earnest. 'If a girl appeals to me then I would observe her carefully over a period to see whether she is suitable,' replied the man I had addressed.

"No one contradicted him. The faces even showed a degree of understanding, if not agreement. At the time the war wasn't yet four years ended.

"I asked myself whether Maria would be repulsed by everything she saw and heard here. I remembered how animated she had been as a schoolgirl, telling me how Prestes's heavily pregnant wife (I hadn't thought of this since) had placed herself protectively in front of her husband when their hiding place was discovered and police officers were rushing towards him. She would understand everything, Maria Luisa, and she would always give the right response in a thick, strange-sounding German, noticeably sharpened from speaking a foreign language.

"As she had only just written to me asking for the love of God to please not send her any money, I agonized over whether I should honor her plea. I was also speculating over the meaning of the words 'if I was suddenly to come'.

"Now she seemed out of reach; now I said to myself quite matter-of-factly that Eliza, who must earn well, will lend her the money.

"I had a lot of work at the time. I also wanted to show Gustav that I had taken his words to heart. On one of my rare visits, my father noticed how pale and thin I had become here. 'Do you still hear from Maria Luisa?' he suddenly asked.

"'Certainly,' I replied. 'Soon she'll come for good.'

"My father was visibly surprised. 'Do you think she'll manage to settle in here, then?' he said. 'She was only a little girl when she went over there.'

"To which I responded: 'Settle in? Together with me?' And I told him all the grounds I had for her imminent arrival, with which I consoled myself lying awake at night from despair.

"Meanwhile, Germany had been divided and the German Democratic Republic established. I certainly didn't yet realize the full significance of these events. Chiefly I thought West Germany would soon follow our example and the division only last a short time. And not just me—the majority of young people around me believed it as firmly. There were so many debates, so much to think about that my time was no longer filled up with fruitless waiting. I also reassured myself that the postal service was disrupted.

"Once the changes were in place and things had settled down a little, I started waiting again. I thought now four, five, six letters would come in a flurry, letters that had been held for me. I sometimes imagined Maria suddenly step into the room. I saw her before me more clearly than ever, a shimmer of gold in her brown hair, eyes ablaze from a life lived every second to the full, her big beautiful mouth. Sometimes I actually shouted: 'Damn you! Why have you made me wait?' And I seized her and smothered her in kisses.

"Then suddenly I was alone. My powers of imagination were spent. Outside, the Berlin night trudged over all the ruins, ruins that would now be rebuilt.

"Yes, the rebuilding had begun. The republic was putting down roots. You no longer heard anyone in the assembly hall say aloud: 'I don't give anything for feelings.' The fact that no one said such things anymore in front of so many people in all openness had its good side and probably also its bad.

"For weeks, months I think, I heard nothing more from Maria Luisa. Somehow I became inured to time. *No letter again*, I thought. Just like any other time, the time without letters drifted by.

"I read her old letters over and over again, searching for a clue as to her prolonged silence. I didn't think of unfaithfulness. To me our belonging together essentially seemed unshakable. But I was afraid of extenuating circumstances, an illness, a change of address, some notion or other of this aunt (who had always seemed unreliable to me).

"I hardly had an evening free. At our meetings and debates we still fought for German unification then. Much later, the clear-cut division of the two separate states was confirmed as something definitive and inevitable.

"Initially, though, many were of the opinion that the development of publicly owned companies was also possible in West Germany.

"I think it was then that people started to ask questions differently to before: who was loyal to the new state and would stand by it? Some students with only one or two years of study to go said (when they knew no one was listening): 'I'll keep my mouth shut. I don't have to decide yet. My degree will be recognized over there too.' But in the passing I also heard workers here and there saying: 'Must dash back—I've given the company a free hour.' Or: 'Ultimately we are the company now. Who would have thought such a thing possible?'

"And because we continued our debates in small groups or in pairs, I stopped losing sleep dwelling on a sorrow far removed from the everyday; because undoubtedly my pain was as before, only it had been forced to retreat deeper inside.

"In the course of the previous year Gustav had become a real friend to me. Ever since I briefly told him that Maria's family was giving her the money for her fare, he no longer asked questions I might have been reluctant to answer. He probably also thought I would now be fully occupied with preparing for my finals.

"I signed up to help with the rebuilding program, removing the mountains of rubble from the city. And where us willing helpers formed chains and passed stones from hand to hand, people often stood speechless or even watched on with derision. I saw Maria Luisa standing nearby, cheerfully, carefully clutching stones. I saw her everywhere. I even made out the detail of her dusty dress.

"I still regularly wrote to her about what happened here, without knowing whether it interested or repulsed her. Because by now a lot of time had passed since she last replied. I didn't dare calculate the length of her silence.

"One day, I received a letter from Rio in an unfamiliar handwriting. I turned it over in my hand with a racing heart. Then it dawned on me: I had probably seen this handwriting before; the letter was from Maria's musical friend, Eliza.

"'Dear Ernesto, you're writing to Maria Luisa as before. She probably hasn't told you what has happened meantime. Maria Luisa simply isn't capable of living alone long-term. I don't mean to say she is head-over-heels in love with Rodolfo, but she has grown fond of him because he always worried about her. His mother has also put pressure on him, particularly after his father's death (from whom he has inherited a lovely house in the Rua Dantas, near the coast). I repeat: Maria Luisa as a whole being was not made to be alone. So she has finally accepted Rodolfo's proposal. I'd say she seems happy now, as though relieved.'

"So I had the information in my hands. The slightest uncertainty would have been bearable compared with a certainty I couldn't endure. Better to wait, fruitlessly wait, weeks and weeks. Now I knew waiting was pointless.

"I told everyone I was sick and locked myself away. When Gustav knocked at my door I didn't answer.

"Suddenly I went to Greifswald, perhaps because my father had known the girl well. 'She's married Rodolfo,' I told him at once.

"'I always suspected,' my father said, 'she would never come here. She cannot live here. You must realize that.'

"My relationship with my father was entirely different to

what is usually the case in our country. We had lived alone together. My mother's death hung constantly like a shadow over us both.

"Now I was no longer waiting for Maria, the most important part of me was missing. I was missing what gave my life its meaning—because my work had had a bearing on Maria, and her proximity on my work. I broke up my purposeless period with various short-lived hopes, for instance waiting for an exam result, even waiting for some girl or other that I liked a little.

"After about a year, I came home to find out of the blue a letter written by Maria Luisa, a long, closely written letter. She said that sometimes in a room full of guests she hears a whistle at the window and then jumps up and runs out, but the street is dark and empty. And sometimes she hears not a whistle but a call. Alone she muses, and now the call comes not from under the window but from the end of the street, the voice shouting: 'Why on earth do you make me wait so long?' or: 'Come, once and for all!' and then she drops everything and runs into town. Ernesto should know, she wrote, that she has traveled a lot lately and spent the night in many a small town.

"In this long, closely written letter it also said: 'We were in Belo Horizonte. You know it as well as me. We drove into the mountains. We went to Congonhas to see Aleijadinho's sculptures. The monk that speaks German so well (remember he told us he was from Bavaria?) showed us around the church. Then he led us down the hill. He showed us the individual pilgrimage points on the stairway. He looked at me and suddenly said: "You no longer have your old travel companion?"

"'No,' I replied. And I said I was now married (this was the first time she mentioned her marriage).

"'I stayed back and sat on a step under the great cloak of one of the prophets. I cried. The monk waited a moment. When I followed on, drying my eyes, he said: "Do not be afraid. You are never alone."

"'Rodolfo, whom I have married—Eliza will have already told you—asked me afterwards: "What did he say to you?" You see, he always has to know what anyone says to me. It occurred to me that he doesn't understand German, and the monk had spoken German with me. So I replied, "Oh, nothing special."

"'We are meanwhile in Bahia for several weeks; for some business reason I understand nothing of. Sleep eludes me. Even when I'm awake, all that comes to mind is what I've seen and heard. But when we are in Rio again, then you'll come out of every door, then I'll hear your constant angry calling.

"'Here too I cannot understand that we are apart. I simply endure it, vacantly, numbly. But in Rio I constantly see you and hear you. Why I can't walk with your hand in my hand, of course I don't understand that there either.'

"The letter stirred me deep inside. I wrote to Maria Luisa asking where I should send the money for her fare. Hardly was this letter sent than I realized she was now a wealthy woman. I immediately wrote a second time: she could leave right away; any further hesitation on her part would only mean agony for us both. But pain prevailed. Because Maria Luisa didn't come; neither did she write a letter. Was she being closely watched? Had she only acted on a feeling in Bahia and written to me in a fit of passion that suddenly came over her and just as suddenly faded…?

"I was sent with a group of students to a cross-trade meeting in Zittau. I was convinced that on my return I would find a letter. But the whole winter long following that November she never wrote. Nor did she write afterwards. She had fallen silent. Perhaps something in one of my letters had greatly angered her. Perhaps she was still traveling with her husband, as far as the Amazon, to Manaus—what do I know. If Maria Luisa was upset, then her husband might have thought of something to distract her from her thoughts. I slowly realized that she wouldn't write so soon.

"Snow lay on the roofs and on the branches. Already the pavements were trampled black. *No snow falls in Brazil,* I thought. *The trees don't shed their leaves. Only one tree is like the trees in the north; the wild almond tree, I think. In a country where everything is different, a person probably changes too. Even Maria Luisa has changed. No. No. Not her.* And what I also thought was (the snow had long melted): *the trees in my part of town are turning green.* They were sparse trees."

*T*he following day, the captain invited us all to dinner. Sadowski told us this is the custom when you cross the equator.

"Are you sure there will be no equator baptism ceremony?" In her anxiety the nun's pale companion at the head of the table, who never said anything, suddenly became animated. She told us that when she made her first crossing the god Poseidon came aboard with mussels sticking to a long beard, and members of the crew grabbed various passengers and dunked them in a disgusting concoction or daubed it on them with long brushes. She said they were in no way reprimanded, that everybody had roared with laughter, but she had found it all very traumatic. And no certificate of baptism (which she later received in recognition of her courageous equator crossing) could console her.

Sadowski listened on with his cunning eyes. You saw how much he enjoyed this account.

"Now then, young lady," he said, "Sister Barbara at any rate is protected from such customs by her nun's habit. Besides, no one need worry this time. Nor are you obliged to drink the schnapps they will hopefully serve us. You may enjoy your evening meal in peace as usual. Alone, even, or with Sister Barbara in case you still don't trust our company. And afterwards, you will still receive a genuine certificate without being smeared in tar or dipped in sludge."

"I don't need it," said the pale, slight little lady, prompted to speak because of the imminent event; "I already have one. I put it in with my travel documents. Yes, so something like that doesn't happen to me again."

"In with your travel documents?" Sadowski enquired, his eyes laughing.

"Why of course, for all eventualities. To prove I need no second baptism."

Sadowski turned to the lady next to him to hide his amusement. Then he told me what he knew: "Now, thirty years ago this little lady traveled to Bahia, to one of the biggest convents there. Not as a nun, but a housekeeper. And she'll probably be sent back again from Poland and on the journey will look after yet another nun held in high regard."

"Is Sister Barbara highly regarded at this convent, then?"

"Seems to be. I often see her sneaking about below between the crew's cabins. Not because she's after a man. She's spoken to as many sailors as she can about a coming religious festival and put them off attending any other event. I sometimes follow her around and listen in."

Old Poseidon with his trident and with mussels in his beard never came onto our ship. They were gentle on us. Not only did we have the nun on board but also people like the famous singer, his wife, and the consulate's wife. Mainly the children might have enjoyed the antics, which they presumably knew from previous journeys. But to celebrate the evening they removed the division. The two passenger tables and the captain's table were moved together.

The captain looked happy and relaxed but in command. When I think back, it was the first time I was really aware of his appearance. And it was the appearance of a man who had sailed munitions to Murmansk eight or nine times during the war.

We pressed him with questions and he told us about these trips, flying in the face of death every time. He spoke at least a few words with each of us. To my amazement he knew about every passenger in detail, far better than Sadowski. He even knew that the old lady (the nanny to the Polish family in Rio who had presented her with multi-colored woolens when saying their goodbyes) had a son who was a building contractor. The old lady wore nothing woolen now. She had on a black dress with a pretty, fringed shawl over it. "I don't know if my son will be able to meet me," she said anxiously.

"We'll put you on the right train," the captain reassured her.

Also on Bartsch's and Triebel's table was a very attractive lady with black hair and gray eyes. I had seen little of her until now because she always had her back to me. Every two years she visited her sister in Brazil. She had already sailed with the *Norwid* once before, in fact with the same captain. He knew her sister's family, as well as her husband, a town planner in Gdansk.

Diagonally opposite me on the captain's side sat my cabin mate, Woytek. That evening, he was clean-shaven and had taken some care over his dress. He didn't join in our conversations. He greedily drank Wiśniówka, the Polish schnapps. I noticed the captain stare at him from time to time. Their eyes met. But Woytek then drank all the more.

Triebel and I wondered what the cook would treat us to for dessert, something Brazilian or Polish. At any rate he offered us an astonishing array of delicious dishes, all kinds of hot and cold meats and fish, and he himself came to serve us and refill our glasses and bask in our praise. He neither laughed nor smiled. He looked like he was lording it. Neither Triebel nor I were right about dessert. There was something enticing from each country: scooped-out pineapples with all the bits brimming over, and golden-yellow baked bananas, and there were shiny red apples that everyone, especially the children, reached for with whoops of joy, and pears dipped in chocolate, the Polish way. Afterwards, there was good coffee and bottles of Wiśniówka which the cook opened before our eyes.

I noticed Woytek's hand already shaking as he reached for

the bottle again. The first officer got there before him to swiftly refill the glass of the lady next to him.

I think it was during dessert that suddenly the ship's whistle loudly blew. The children nudged each other and leapt up to look out. "There's nothing to see at the equator," the captain laughed.

Whether from excitement or because now he thought no one was watching, Woytek had a very quick drink. And just after that—we were all quietly enjoying the aroma of coffee, the cabin brightly lit by the sun lowering over the ocean—Woytek shouted: "I don't want to! I don't want to!"

The captain turned sharply to him. He gave some sort of order which really shut him up. Choking from his outburst, Woytek proceeded to tear off his collar and tie, then his jacket and shirt. The first officer stood up and grabbed him, but before he could overpower him two of the crew came in. "Klebs!" the first officer commanded. And this Klebs, though slight of build, almost weak-looking, grabbed Woytek in a vice-like grip. They both dragged him out. You saw from their faces that they were used to it.

"Hopefully not to our cabin," I muttered.

"That's why we have a sick room," someone replied.

The passengers all looked perturbed. I now feared for the lovely party, when the singer stood up and broke the stunned silence by asking unassumingly if he might sing a song. Everyone was glad at the suggestion. There and then we shook off this image of a crazed Woytek. We listened closely as the singer explained almost at a hush: "My friend has set to music my favorite poems of Norwid—Cyprian Norwid, after whom our ship is named. I will sing one for you."

I never imagined that the small, sedate man who had sat opposite me for the best part of a week would be capable of such a thing. Now I understood why his countrymen and women in the concert hall in Rio had wept. And I also understood why his country had sent him out like a messenger. His little wife looked up at him with pride.

After the song, which marked the close of our dinner party, we milled around here and there. Suddenly the singer came up to Triebel and me, bearing his little book: "I must give you some idea of this poet," he said. The singer spoke German well. His voice also sounded good reciting. He translated a few verses for us:

> "Oh Lord, I long for that land where every breadcrumb
> that falls to the ground is picked up reverently.
> I long for the land where it is seen as a sin
> to destroy a stork's nest in a pear tree,
> because it belongs to everyone.
> I long for that land.
> I long for other things too:
> for people whose 'yes' means 'yes' and 'no' means 'no',
> and who differentiate light from shade.
> Where someone cares for me.
> And so it must be, because I leave no friend.
> I long to be there, oh Lord!"

The singer's wife was quiet and friendly. She told us that they always had the little book in their suitcase. How pleased they were that the ship bore his name!

The passengers looked out for Triebel and me. They left us to our sheltered, shaded spot under the steps, even when Triebel in his excitement suddenly started to pace up and down for minutes at a time.

It was apparent that Triebel's talking and my listening had become an integral part of the crossing for them. And if to begin with I was surprised that Triebel should pour out his heart to me, a stranger, now I was eager to know how his story continued. I found he had been right to tell it to me in particular.

"You have to understand," he said, "that Maria's last letter, and my waiting after her letters dried up altogether, more facilitated than disrupted my studies. It was as though I had made my maxim a desperate 'now more than ever'.

"I had already chosen a topic from internal medicine for my future doctoral thesis. Above all, I found I could master time studying and learning. Perhaps unconsciously I reckoned with one day facing time's grim interminable hand alone, while still counting on the miracle that Maria Luisa could suddenly walk into my room, having traveled here secretly, having come to me, and I, meanwhile I would have come a long way.

"By no means did I give up with attempts to pick up her trail. I remembered such and such a friend from schooldays and wrote to each, would they get in touch and let me know how they were, and casually asked if they had seen Maria. Those I wrote to replied fairly quickly. They probably realized the matter was important to me. However, none had seen Maria lately. One said she had moved to another city, to Pernambuco his brother-in-law told him; another even said she had gone to the United States. At the same time they told me various other things, for instance that Vargas had become president a second time, that it appeared he now intended to use entirely different, virtually liberal methods of governance. They said he had unexpectedly granted release to some prisoners. They also wrote about things that were of no interest to me whatsoever, for instance Eliza having gone to various countries on a concert tour. At the mention of Maria's absence, one more friend added that Aunt Elfriede (whom no doubt I would remember) no longer worked in the clothes shop. Now Rodolfo would probably see her right in old age. In any case this friend had heard nothing of Maria Luisa in two years. The other thought he had seen her a few weeks ago, very smartly dressed, greeting him amiably with a familiar smile as she got out of a fancy car, a Chevrolet. As far as he knew she lived mainly in the house Rodolfo had inherited from his father.

"It was only natural that I fell for some girl, a fellow student. Perhaps to outsiders I seemed blissfully in love and the girl happy too. I openly tell you that I'm still friends with one such very young girl. Friends. That's all; because with this girl, just as with the others, the moment always arrived when they asked: 'Why don't you tell me everything? I feel you're hiding something. *Something*, do you know what I mean?' If pressed too much I replied: 'Alright, for years I've been attached to a woman. It's well-nigh impossible she'll come, but I can't break the waiting habit. Please don't ask anything more.' The relationship usually then dissolved of its own accord.

"By now the Stockholm Appeal had coursed through the world. South Korea had been invaded. The second Peace

Congress had taken place in Warsaw. And in '51, in August, there was a great celebration in Berlin for young people and students. Gustav, who remained my friend (he studied economics and would graduate that year), was glad at my collaborating at every opportunity. He wasn't one to ask what became of the great love of my life which had preoccupied me long after my arrival. I would have dodged the question, or I would have had to say: I'm still waiting. Would he then have asked, aghast: 'Still?'

"Perhaps only my father had some idea of my ineradicable hope. Because when I visited he never asked. And from this same silence I sensed he knew. Only once, when I went to him for advice about a relatively rare kidney complaint, did he say, smiling: 'Did Theodosio, the cobbler, not once have a similar condition and you two asked me to help him?' We were silent some minutes. He must have been studying my face because suddenly he said: 'I would think Maria Luisa has a child by now. She'll be completely absorbed with it.'

"I said nothing to this and thought nothing either.

"By now I had my own room, and one day a medical practitioner by the name of Heinz Schulz appeared at mine. We had lived together a long time in our student house. He was a little older than me. He was a surgical assistant.

"'I tell you why I'm looking for you for,' he said: 'my professor has a friend, a Professor Dahlke from Leipzig. A world famous anatomist, you know. He's likely the first German one to be invited abroad since the war, namely to the big medical trade fair in São Paulo. Now you see where the wind blows, my dear chap. I take it you still want to see Brazil again and the good friends you have there. This Professor Dahlke needs an interpreter, if possible one who is also a doctor. Because you'll take with you to São Paulo—this could complicate your journey, but you needn't worry—a model of a lady made of glass with all the internal organs, which can be lit up electrically. A complex, collaborative, exquisitely executed operation by doctors and technicians. Dahlke, I heard him talk with my professor, to begin with he was frankly furious about this glass lady he is entrusted with. But eventually he calmed down. Perhaps he's realized that an exhibition piece like this will be of scientific, therefore also political, benefit. When he insisted upon a suitable travel companion I immediately thought of you. I've put my recommendation to my professor. So if you say yes, everything will be in order.'

"I said yes. I thanked him. I kept in check the emotions that instantly welled up: agonizing joy, equally agonizing fear. Would I really get to see Maria again soon? Where? How? Would we find words?

"I was introduced to Dahlke. He gave the impression of someone very arrogant and full of himself who, like a monarch presenting a loyal front to his people, concealed his arrogance and attempted to come down to my level by being jokey and amenable.

"Together we inspected the glass lady. Dahlke had to introduce her at the exhibition and I translate his explanations, so we turned on the electric lighting and determined how best to describe everything to visitors. We had many a good laugh during these try-outs. Dahlke lost his pomposity. He said he was only angry at being treated like a circus act here. I reassured him the glass figure was a technological wonder and told him about the first-rate doctors over there, many of whom had been friends of my father. We could do something for science, I told him; aside from the intelligentsia, all kinds of people were poised to come to the exhibition, ignorant people, prejudiced people.

"Dahlke nodded with the smile of adults listening to the hopes of the young.

"The glass lady was packed in a crate under our supervision. We gave our solemn promise to guard her with the utmost diligence. *This promise primarily falls on my shoulders*, I thought, because Dahlke didn't give the impression he needed constant reassurance over the safe storage of our baggage. In fact he had initially planned to fly by plane, but suddenly changed his mind. He himself was taking a lot of stuff, medical books and equipment which he had promised to friends. He said that all this luggage was far too expensive for the plane; at the end of the day he couldn't expect our state to be liable for all his personal needs.

"As promised, I kept an eye on the crate with the glass model. I paid less attention to Professor Dahlke, his luggage, and his conversation.

"Crates and cases came with us. First to Warsaw, because from Warsaw we then had to go to Gdynia, as our ship was lying there. In Warsaw I had to arrange our onward journey and the shipping of our glass lady. As a result, I hardly saw the city. However, I didn't deprive myself of seeing the monument erected in honor of the Warsaw Uprising and the memorial for the Ghetto Uprising. Because all the horror of the ghetto went up in flames and burnt down during the uprising. Here I must add that when we visited Warsaw—black as the inside of a mine after the German army incinerated and leveled it—the greater part of the city had been rebuilt. Although no ruins remained on the area of the ghetto where the memorial stands, or any of its original traces, it wasn't yet covered in houses and gardens as is the case today. It was an oppressive wasteland and as such allowed no room to forget.

"I have to say, that night as I visited the memorial sites for the Warsaw uprisings, I completely forgot about myself. I was made to think about war atrocities that bore witness to the Nazi regime and the war, but more than that, these were the most extreme of atrocities which at the same time provided the most profound proof that all wickedness sooner or later meets with resistance and is ended.

"No, during those few hours I no longer thought about myself. To no longer think about myself also meant to forget everything concerning me: our journey's destination and even my love for Maria Luisa.

"But when I say I forgot my love for her, you shouldn't take that to mean I completely wiped Maria Luisa from my thoughts and feelings, oh no, just my painful ruminating ceased, as though quite unworthy of these places. It seemed she walked with me, hand in hand. We were both silent and moved as young people in particular can be.

"We were there for such a short time, Dahlke and I, that I wasn't able to see anything else. Only Dahlke walked around. He later told me all about the admirable rebuilding process. If I remember rightly, he also spoke regrettably about how much suffering the Germans had inflicted on other nations. I don't want to do him an injustice, Dahlke. He was an officer in the war. It may be he himself inflicted some of that suffering.

"We went with our crates to Gydnia. I inspected the ship's exterior with a seaman's eye. I had come to Europe on a French one. Like our *Norwid*, this was a cargo ship with several cabins for passengers. She was almost new and gleamed white. I liked the look of her. We had a different captain and first officer but the same cook, which is strange.

"From the moment we were aboard Dahlke became talkative, even in port. I sensed he was elated as we departed.

"You have to appreciate that I myself was in a state of nervous excitement, so wasn't interested in Dahlke's questions. Whatever he did or didn't do went on behind my back. There was no trace left of the feeling that Maria Luisa accompanied me. *They're bound to read the passenger list*, I thought. *Rodolfo is a businessman; they will know now that Dahlke and Triebel are arriving soon. Will she meet me? Will she avoid me? Will she go back with me?*

"Dahlke was very happy with his cabin. He quickly made friends—he spoke excellent English. All the same he in no way ignored me, even though I would rather just have been left to my anticipation. But not only did Dahlke want to know all about Rio and São Paulo, he also asked about Montevideo and other Latin American capital cities. When I think now, neither of us gave due attention to the incredible journey itself—through Kattegat and Skagerrak and then southwards to Antwerp—or to each other, because we were each wrapped up in our own particular sense of anticipation.

"I later reproached myself for not being more mindful of my travel companion, but they reassured me once I was back home—and home for me is now undoubtedly the country I live and work in—that I could not have changed either his mind or his intentions. The only thing that has stayed with me from the entire journey is that, not far from the Danish coast, someone pointed out a castle on a peninsula and claimed that this was where the ghost of Hamlet's father appeared to Hamlet.

"Dahlke (who often visited me) came into my cabin again now and asked me with a strange smile if I was keen on ghosts.

"'Ghosts, no; creatures made of flesh and blood,' I replied.

"'Oh yes, your friend said you have people in Brazil who are very dear to you.'

"I merely replied, 'Indeed,' and I thought: *what has that got to do with you?*

"But throughout the entire lengthy journey he often made similar allusions. He also said: 'It must have been hard for you to settle in Berlin.' Or: 'Were you able to get used to Germany?'

"I responded a dozen times that the main things for me were my work and good friends. During these conversations he would give me a searching look, almost on tenterhooks, as though he had asked something sensitive, although surely it was all one to him what I felt.

"In Antwerp the ship picked up I don't know how many crates of screws and nails and different tools for precision engineering. I spent most of the time in a cargo hold ensuring nothing happened to our own crate. Besides, I didn't have the papers to leave the ship and walk around on Belgian soil.

"When I returned on deck, I was amazed to learn that

Dahlke had received a visitor and obtained permission to accompany him to a café.

"From Antwerp we sailed out into open sea.

"There's not much to tell about that crossing. It was largely the same as the one we are now making in the opposite direction. Only I was filled with uncertainty and anxiety. I can tell you everything now, Franz Hammer; I know how it's turned out, I well-nigh know, and look, since I'm being open with you—God knows why I'm being open with you in particular—all will become fully clear to me in the telling. You already more or less know why...

"On the evening before our departure—I mean this last one when we met, you and I—once more, one last time I was shaken by an encounter. I would be lying if I claimed that now at last everything was clear to me. Please tell me what you yourself make of this incident; it's likely the conclusion to everything I've told you on the journey—as long as I'm not holding you back; you must want to talk lots with other people?"

"I've time enough, Triebel, to talk with the others all day long," I told him truthfully. "And anyway, now I really want to know what happened with your Maria Luisa."

"As the journey neared its end, Dahlke was no longer as eager to talk to me. He had made any number of friends with passengers who spoke English well. The things that have captivated us over these days—you, Hammer, and me, and the others, Bartsch for instance—the stars in the sky and the fish flying over the sea, none of it even registered with Dahlke. But periodically he came up to me to ask obscure facts about the country, and I was surprised to note that his mood and in turn his behavior had completely altered.

"The nearer our arrival, the harder I was finding it in the form of something like arrival angst, as well as strange inexplicable misgiving. And Dahlke was all the more jovial, all the more animated the closer we came to land.

"During the night, we sailed past the massive island, veiled in mist, which you also know now. When I told Dahlke it was sort of a sentinel guarding Brazil, he rubbed his hands with glee. I didn't like that gesture one bit. Otherwise, I thought nothing more. I was drained from anticipation."

Suddenly the Polish children came running up to us, with no heed for Triebel's arresting account. Happily they shouted something we couldn't quite understand. They simply would not allow Triebel to continue. They grabbed us by the hand and pulled us with them.

Various passengers were already standing at the ship's bow, looking at the water with smiles of wonder. A big pod of dolphins had started to accompany us. Their faces straining out of the water, they regarded us with smiling eyes and laughing mouths, as though willing us to join their fun, and at the same time to see who their fellow travelers were on this particular ship. They were as fast as us and could have gone faster with ease because as they accompanied us they were having fun racing each other or playfully spurring each other on. And time and again they looked up at us. They reminded me of a pack of young hounds given the treat of jumping into the water.

It made me as happy as—who knows why, for what reason—the dolphins were. Now I was wholeheartedly in agreement with my sea journey. It went through my head that I would never have seen anything like this driving in the mountains with my family.

They live at sea and dive in and out of the water yet have faces that are perhaps more honest than the faces of many human beings, for instance this Dahlke whom Triebel had been telling me about. And for a fleeting moment I even thought about what had brought me to be on this ship: my colleagues' oversight and then the long, tedious journey to Rio Grande do Sul. It had just been one of those things. Now, in my delight, I forgot the down sides. I wished this pod of dolphins would never leave our ship.

But after a few minutes they all disappeared together into the sea; perhaps one dolphin had given a signal. Triebel sighed happily once more. His face too looked different. We stared at the water a while. It looked lonely and empty. There was nothing else left but to go back to our usual spot under the steps.

Once there, Triebel continued: "We docked at Rio. As we entered port, Dahlke, who was in ebullient mood anyway, pointed out with great enthusiasm all the marvels and wonders, as though it was my first time here.

"As the gangway was lowered, filled with trepidation I scanned the docking area. But I knew that only in exceptional cases could a passenger be met here. At any rate the interpreter who the exhibition organizing committee had sent was waiting. He was surprised I could speak Portuguese as well as him. He explained that the overnight train would take us with our crate to São Paulo. He was a polite little swarthy man. He went straight with us to customs, *alfândega*. The vast hall teemed with people of every color and provenance, as in my childhood, as though ships had never stopped arriving—and neither had they. We had to wait the best part of an hour for our luggage because clearly we were without my wily old uncle who would have hurried everything along. Because 'Care when opening!' was written so glaringly on the long, coffin-like crate in German, Portuguese, Polish and every other language under the sun, the customs officials just had to see what was inside. But they lifted up the lid slowly and carefully. They greeted a glimmer of the lady with 'oohs' and 'aahs'. They didn't dare touch her glass limbs.

"Meanwhile, a well dressed, European-looking man with gray hair had entered our group. I gave no heed to his welcome, which anyway was for Dahlke alone. Dahlke muttered that the gentleman was a relative.

"Something else had caught my attention. Amidst countless people bustling between customs desks, suitcases and crates, an elderly woman had surfaced, obviously local, not newly arrived. She was dressed in gray. She didn't linger in one specific spot awaiting luggage. She flitted about much more like a bat, from one place to the next, wherever her claws gripped. From the moment I looked around the monstrous customs hall, my eyes were drawn almost automatically to this lady, also from the way she carried herself; something about her struck me as familiar.

"At the same time, I kept checking to make sure our crate was being properly closed, because by now Doctor Dahlke was exclusively occupied with his relative. When I next looked up, almost immediately this gray lady caught my eye. She was circling between all manner of new arrivals, in and out of groups of monks and curious crowds of builders and farmers. And I saw she was circling ever closer round us in particular, until finally there was no doubt: her eyes sought me.

"Rather than simply come up and talk to me as Doctor Dahlke's relative had confidently done, from a certain distance she indicated that she wished to speak with me. Suddenly I remembered where I knew her from: it was Emma, the German housemaid who had worked for Aunt Elfriede after Odilia's dismissal.

"When she was finally within hearing distance I shouted: 'It's you, Emma! Emma, what have you to say to me?'

"'Yes, Herr Ernesto, it's me. It's imperative I speak with you,' she replied diffidently and decisively at once.

"'But,' I said, 'we're going to the big trade fair in São Paulo pretty much right away.'

"'Then I'll come and pick you up there tomorrow. I must speak with you as soon as possible,' she replied.

"'Where is Maria Luisa?' I could contain myself no longer.

"Turning to me again as now she walked away, she gloomily replied: 'Where would she be? With God in Heaven. I'll tell you everything tomorrow.'

"She was gone so fast I wondered if the encounter had actually taken place.

"Her words slowly sank in. I felt no uncontrollable pain. It struck me that I had known what was in store for me. When I agreed to this trip, something sinister lay ahead. My thought had been: *something awaits me on arrival that can no longer be put right.*

"Now it had come true and the emptiness was conclusive, as previously with Eliza's message that Maria would never come. No—then there was still perhaps the notion of a future turnaround, of renewed contact, which you do not abandon as long as the person you love is alive.

"At the same time I suppose I chatted with those around me, the customs officials, the interpreter, Dahlke. And I felt a growing anticipation to hear Emma's account. When I heard what Emma knew, I would see Maria Luisa before me. If she really was dead, then she would be less dead.

"After leaving customs, the representative from the trade fair took us to the nearest restaurant. It was a *churrascaria*, a steak house. The age-old yet fresh smell of sizzling, searing meat really got to me. I stood and went over to the fire a moment and then, forcibly shaking off my pain and anguish, I went out onto the street for a minute. I had to do it; I had to breathe in the smell of fruit from the nearest stall. I almost went numb because the smell brought flooding back everything I had forgotten: how I had gone shopping with the schoolgirl at the market for the first time, how she prepared a dish from avocados for my father and me, and even all the stops we made on the way to Congonhas, the ragged black children with their sliced oranges. You'll find it hard to understand; I breathed it all in and understood for the first time: she will never breathe it all in again.

"I went back to our table. The others were almost finished their meal. The interpreter had ordered a big plate of different kinds of fruit for us. Dahlke was clumsily peeling a mango. I felt such irrational jealousy over a single piece of fruit from that country that I could have ripped it from his fingers.

"We traveled overnight to São Paulo. The exhibition was a world of color and confusion within a wider world which is nevertheless yet to be surpassed for its color and confusion. Hardly was she freed from her packaging, our glass lady, lit by electric light, drew an unbelievable number of people. I handed out my brochures. Various visitors studied them and then checked on our glass figure whether the kidneys, intestines, heart and lungs were in the right places. Others simply stared at the lady, completely overwhelmed.

"We had the occasional laugh, Dahlke and I. We watched a couple of young boys in shock at the realization that the girls they smothered in kisses were created like this inside and no differently. Unfortunately I didn't pay much attention to Dahlke.

"In the afternoon, Emma's gloomy face surfaced in the crowd. She only gave a cursory glance at our exhibit. It was all the same to her whether the lady was transparent or made of flesh and blood.

"She waited until the lights had been switched off and the visitors had dispersed. Then she had to further wait until our lady was packed away and entrusted to the night watchman.

"I invited Emma to dinner, but she had already dined with relatives. She would travel back that night. She had taken the day off. She told me Frau Altmeier (that was Aunt Elfriede, whom Emma still referred to by her surname) lived in another part of town since giving up the shop.

"'I am at a hotel,' Emma said. 'I like it better than private employers. What bother I had with you two, for instance! Now my cousin can stand in for me when I want.'

"I remembered how we had disliked this Emma. Nevertheless, she quickly became indispensable to us, as a messenger and go-between.

"I had already had a few glasses when Emma slowly, dolefully began: 'My boss always gets a list containing most of the new arrivals, so last week he called me over: "Emma, have a look and see if you know these two, Dahlke and Triebel. They're coming to São Paulo, to the trade fair."

"'My dear Herr Ernesto, I don't even have to tell you what your leaving meant for Maria Luisa. Being alone—that was hell for Maria Luisa. Me, for instance, I've been alone all my days. I'm not used to company.

"'When you left, Maria Luisa lay there without crying, without calling your name, completely paralyzed. Not just for hours—for days. Eventually her aunt—who had not a clue what to do and feared for the girl's life—called Eliza round to the house. Herr Ernesto, do you still remember Eliza, who was her friend?

"'"You've no piano here," Eliza said. "You're coming to my house right away so I can play you all my favorite new pieces. No nonsense now. There's dinner at ours anyway, and I've invited a few more friends round to listen."

"'From then on Maria often went to her friend Eliza's.

"'Rodolfo was usually among the guests. As you know, he always worshipped Maria Luisa. She didn't want to know about him—because of you. Sometimes he stood outside our door into the night. All the flowers and quite unbelievable gifts he sent her! She just laughed about it—because of you. Then she often went round to her friend's in the evening.

"'All the same she waited dreadfully for your letters. She would run to the post office and ask if a letter had been left lying somewhere. When a letter arrived in your handwriting she greedily, thirstily read every word, even the address. Then she threw herself onto her bed.

"'When I asked her once, "So what will happen now—will you go to him, or will he come back here?" it spilled out, slowly at first, then faster and faster, finally in a furious flood she told me everything, me alone, because she had no one else to speak to unreservedly. Apparently Eliza wasn't the right person, or her aunt, let alone Rodolfo. She probably just needed to express herself in German. "Who knows if we'll see each other again! Where is he meant to get all this money so he can come to me, or to send me so that I can go to him? These plans we made— we were kidding ourselves. But he still firmly believes we'll see each other again, soon even. And when I read his letters, his beautiful believable letters, I almost begin to believe our seeing each other again is imminent."

"'But days passed. Weeks went by, months too, until they made a year. And as in a dream a year turned into another and, without anyone wishing it, the third year was there.

"'My dear Herr Ernesto, I'm sure you know being alone was torture for Maria Luisa. Many a time she flung open the door and cried: "Ernesto!"

"'I will say no more about that time. I think in the end she was convinced there was just no way for you to come to her, or she to you... should I really tell you everything, Herr Ernesto?'"

"'Definitely; tell it all, all according to the truth,'" I said to her.

"'Suddenly Rodolfo and Maria were standing before me. She had her arm around Rodolfo's neck. She was beaming, or gave that impression. "You are the first we're letting in on a secret. We are engaged," she said.

"'Although, dear Herr Ernesto, I always doubted you would come, I stared at Maria Luisa as though she had gone mad—because she was your bride, yours alone, before God and the people. Anything otherwise was impossible. Rather than money for her fare Rodolfo gave his inheritance as dowry, the house in Rua Dantas.

"'"Every night utterly alone," she said once; "And how many nights more?" From then on she never spoke like that again. But I often heard her crying bitterly—only at night. As though now she knew what loneliness was for. Yes, she cried bitterly even after the engagement.

"'Still she showed me your letters. Once, she said: "If I'm going to go then it must be now, right away. Eliza would lend me the money for the journey, seeing as Ernesto will soon send her it. Do you not think? Honestly, I'll just go."

"'I was not convinced Eliza would lend her money. But I was pleased she had renewed hope of your seeing each other again. Then she stopped showing me your letters. As she read, her face visibly darkened. Once, she cried out: "This guy doesn't know what's possible or how it can be achieved!"

"'I went to the wedding to see her in all her loveliness. Usually I don't set store by beauty but I loved Maria Luisa as my own. Her face was white as snow. There's no snow here—as the flowers in her hair, then. She rightfully wore the wedding wreath.

"'After the wedding, I helped Maria a lot in the newly-refurbished house in Rua Dantas. I also slept there when she went away on a trip with her husband (which happened quite often) and when we had to prepare something fine for guests. A well-run house was very important to Herr Rodolfo. Maria Luisa quickly acclimatized. I cannot remember her crying after her wedding. No, she didn't cry again.

"'But some time later she sat down beside me in the corner by the cupboard—this had been her favorite place before as well—and out of the blue said softly but fiercely: "Oh, Emma, if I didn't have you, you who know all the past. My life now is hard to bear."

"'"Have you not jewelry enough that you can sell?" I said to her. "Secretly? Can you not just go to him? Or have him come to you?"

"'"Oh, Emma!" she replied. "Do you not know the laws in this country? There's no divorce here. They wouldn't even issue me with a ticket without Rodolfo's permission; and if he's here and I'm Rodolfo's wife—what a life that would be!"

"'Again she started to wait for your letters, like before. I made sure Rodolfo didn't snatch them away.

"'Ernesto—why did you not come?

"'Once, her husband insisted on a big dinner party. I

could tell Maria Luisa detested all these guests Rodolfo was set on inviting. After all, he was a businessman and wanted to entertain the people who gave him business. Maria Luisa refused. Then she gave in. We prepared a feast. Maria Luisa was beautifully dressed. She wore gold. She looked like the figures in the churches in Belo Horizonte. She asked me to stay at the house and sleep there afterwards as well because, after parties like these, you know what it's like, there's always a hellish mess. As for me though, being used to the hotel industry, I just clear it up again in no time, no skin off my nose. Whoosh! And it's nice and tidy like before.

"'So I stayed at the house for Maria. I thought she would lie in, but no. The next morning, she appeared in the kitchen as early as usual, bathing costume under her arm. "Emma, I'm quickly going for a dip," she said. "Please put the coffee on meantime. We'll have it here at the kitchen table, like before."

"'She was hardly gone twenty minutes—I'm sure you know that the Rua Dantas backs directly onto the beach—when all these strange people came rushing into the house. Is this where the beautiful lady lives? And a moment later they brought in Maria Luisa. Oh Lord, my God! She had been washed ashore. She wasn't visibly hurt. Only she was as white as at her wedding.

"'The people argued whether she had simply drowned and then been tossed ashore, or been thrown against rocks by the waves.

"'She was dead, the child I loved as my own—although I have no child of my own. I can't imagine anyone loving their own child as I loved Maria Luisa.

"'You of all people, Herr Ernesto, must see that this was no coincidence. She leaves the house early in the morning and doesn't come back alive. Certainly some rocks are steep. There are flat areas too, which the young ones sometimes like to slide along into the water to swim. Many also swim in and out of the rocks into open water.

"'And Maria Luisa knew her way around. She knew exactly where there were currents. She deliberately chose the place she required.

"'Why did you not come in time, Ernesto? Maybe "in time" would have been two years ago, I mean, two years before her death—when you suddenly come, now that it's too late. But the fact that you're here shows you could have come if need be.'

"With these last, devastating words Emma stood up. She even cast a cursory glance at her wristwatch. This seemed to be her way, to save things of consequence until last, until she was leaving. She limply gave me her hand. However, I took another step over to the door and asked her where Eliza lived now. 'In the suburbs; she has a house and a garden.'

"Although Emma had been so dry with me and I had considered her incapable of any feeling, she had been adept at making me aware of my guilt, once and for all.

"I don't know how I got through the days at the exhibition after Emma's account. I translated Dahlke's explanations, added bits here and there, I handed out brochures. At the end of the week the exhibition organizing committee invited us to a farewell dinner. A sightseeing tour of São Paulo was also planned for the exhibition's major contributors, and a trip to the countryside, to a large farm, so we could see how coffee was grown and how it was harvested and roasted. Afterwards, there would be the usual hearty lunch of simple fare at the farm and as much coffee as everyone wanted.

"I hadn't the slightest desire to join in. Although I had no particular affection for Eliza, I wanted to call on her before I left because I would never have another opportunity to see the girl. Besides, as a young boy I had gone with classmates to visit their relatives' coffee plantations. I was familiar with the bushes the coffee beans grew on, some already ripe, others blossoming like in spring; I was familiar with the smell of sieving and roasting, and the villages' singing that harked back to the slave trade, just like the manor house built in the colonial style, well-preserved in the main.

"I excused myself, saying I had to visit people in Rio before I left. Then I asked the porters to pack away our glass lady. I watched on closely as they did, but was completely taken aback when Professor Dahlke suddenly came up to me and, quite frankly, proceeded to verbally attack me. What was the idea in carting away the crate? Various gentlemen have requested a private viewing of one or two exhibits again in peace, he shouted. What's more, he had given his word of honor in Berlin never to be separated from the object.

"I could never have imagined Dahlke would completely lose the rag and tell me off like a little schoolboy. His behavior seemed extraordinary, wholly inadmissible and to a certain extent suspicious, although I didn't spot the reason. Fortunately, pushed for time my porters had nailed shut the long crate without paying heed to Dahlke's angry outburst.

"Yes, as Dahlke, red in the face and spluttering with rage demanded the crate be unloaded or transferred, it was already on its way to the train station, possibly even already on the train from São Paulo to Rio, according to my instructions. I informed Dahlke of this in a slightly mocking manner, and casually but cuttingly demanded he changed his tune with me because, as you probably know, when we suffer greatly we are immune to rudeness, unpleasantness and stupidity. *Perhaps he'll make a complaint about me back in Berlin*, I thought fleetingly. *That is the least of my worries.*

"Then I set off hurriedly for the train.

"Previously Eliza lived not far from Maria and me, on a street parallel to the Rua Catete, in one of those strange, tall narrow houses that looked as though people from imperial times still lived there. Eliza had waited for us on her balcony stuck on the front with no room to sit, only stand.

"Now she lived in the district of Ipanema. Her little house looked appealing. It had no garden as such, as I had envisaged from Emma's description, more a front lawn hidden from the street by high railings. Bougainvillea grew up against the house. Between small blossoming almond trees was a table and chairs all freshly laid, ready for visitors. When I opened the garden gate, rather than a ringing, an unusual melody began, which lured me further in and melted away my unease.

"Eliza looked the same as ever, only she was meticulously dressed. Here in this country, you often come across people with a distinctive beauty that stems from a mixing of various races. I don't know what mix Eliza's family consisted of. I had her in my memory as ugly, and on first appearances her ugliness seemed undiminished. Her cheek and collarbones protruded markedly. There was no trace of goodness or charity to mitigate

Eliza's visible harshness. *But yet, when she plays, you think to hear a magical being*, I thought. I do her an injustice, then.

"I sat down at the garden table. She offered me schnapps and sweets. I ruefully regarded her lovely slender hands. It was she who then began: 'You haven't changed, Ernesto. No doubt you've come to talk about old times. We were all such happy school children. But the luck didn't last for us all—even if I can't complain myself.'

"'Yes, you're right,' I replied. 'I've come to talk one more time about Maria Luisa. Emma, Frau Elfriede Altmeier's former housemaid, has told me everything.'

"'Then I'm spared from describing the accident to you again in all its detail.'

"'Had I only come sooner, Eliza! We would have found a way out. This marriage wouldn't have happened, had I come in time. She wouldn't have ended her life out of despair. What's the sense in speaking about my own pain, about how I will forever reproach myself? Maria Luisa has ended her wonderful, precious life. That would never have happened had she and I got together in time. I do not understand how time can be so treacherous.'

"Eliza sat up: 'Ernesto, what are you talking about? Who put it into your head that Maria Luisa ended her own life? Who dished you up this suicide story? Not Emma, by any chance? She always did enjoy her confusion and fabrication.

"'I'm going to tell you something now, Ernesto, in the danger that you won't altogether like what you hear. The day before she drowned in a tragic accident—at a spot where many have drowned before—there was a party at Rodolfo's house. I too was a guest. Maria Luisa looked lovely beyond compare. "Eliza, how happy I am!" she whispered. Maybe a week previously she had said to me: "I never knew what happiness was, Eliza. I didn't know what true love was, so I didn't know what happiness was either. Do you remember Ernesto? Okay, so we were friends. Our friendship from school lasted a long, long time. Far too long, I realize now. But my life with Rodolfo now, this is no school friendship; this is joy, pure joy." She put her arm around me and said: "Never in my wildest dreams could I have imagined that something this wonderful was possible."

"'And now someone claims she thought to kill herself. That's just lies and nonsense. Perhaps my words hurt you. The truth prevails. No, Ernesto, it was an accident. Even though it hurts, my dear, you must take comfort in the thought that she never believed to find her happiness in life with you. And me, I'm letting you know the whole truth, that's just how I am. You suffer more from a lie than from the brutal truth.'

"I was silent, completely confused. 'I want to show you my house,' she said then. And she led me in the front door and through several rooms. I hardly took in my surroundings. She sat down at the piano, once, twice, played for a minute and I listened on in bewilderment.

"Then I went to my hotel.

"I found a letter waiting for me. I couldn't think whose handwriting it was. I looked down at the signature: Adalbert Dahlke.

"I was a bit baffled by the fairly lengthy letter. At first glance I thought it might be connected with the harsh words we had recently exchanged in São Paulo. But I quickly realized what the letter meant. Dahlke wrote that I should not be put out by his taking leave of me in this fashion; he really had no other option. What's more, saying goodbye in person could have had awkward repercussions for me. I would have had to dissuade him (and that would have been pointless) or I would have gone with him. But he had already seen on the journey that, unfortunately, such a thing was out of the question for me. He had accepted a professorship in Montevideo but in all likelihood would go to the United States within the year, as soon as his contract there was sorted. He wished me a safe journey home and—because, after all, I wished it thus—also a good future in the country I had chosen for my career.

"Now I understood why Dahlke had been so set on carrying off the glass lady to Montevideo. Undoubtedly he would have liked to take her with him to his new teaching posts, which explained why he had been so livid with me for taking her to Rio.

"On the journey back I didn't think of Dahlke for a moment. I thought of my conversations with Emma and Eliza. I would never find out whether Emma's story was based on the truth. But I felt that Eliza had intended ill with her venomous version of events, something I never, ever forgot. Yet her words had made no impression on me. Because I possessed a pledge which I had revealed nothing about, either to Eliza or to Emma: Maria's letter, long after she was married, describing how she really felt inside. For days during the journey home I thought of Maria Luisa with indestructible love, with profound sadness. And later too, these feelings stayed with me as the very essence of all my thoughts and actions.

"Once again the journey home unfolded on a ship, on account of my luggage, the glass lady."

The ship's mate who always announced the meals stood directly behind us and rang the gong in our ears, as though we were hard of hearing. I took Triebel by the arm to bring him to dinner. As we went he found time to say: "Everything would be fine if we could talk of a story that ends in death. But my story isn't finished yet. Forgive me, Hammer, I have to tell you absolutely everything, if only for the sake of closure, which will come after the end, after what I've long taken to be the end. I want to hear your opinion; perhaps so I can ease my mind, ease it a little, for a time. To be honest, I've partly told you everything, the real end to this whole lengthy episode. But the real end came the day before you and I set sail, as I've told you several times already. The last part of my story shouldn't take long because it's the conclusion. I will never stop thinking about it, though. But first I want to hear your opinion, Franz Hammer. We still have a good part of the journey to go, so I've time, if you will allow me."

"Allow you?" I said. "What you have told me up till now has greatly affected me. And if you say the real conclusion is yet to come and if I can in some way help you with my own opinion, then I want to know everything, that's for certain."

We sat down at our respective tables. I heard Bartsch say to Triebel: "Let's go onto the bridge tonight. I've carefully noted down which constellations will move into our night sky in place of the southern constellations."

I asked if I could come. "How can you ask such a thing?" Bartsch laughed. "Now, you know, doing some work or during an experiment or when listening to someone, you can be attuned to a particular person. Then a third is a disruption. No, Hammer, you're certainly not disturbing us. Not us, and not the Great Bear either."

That night on the bridge, Bartsch showed us that the Southern Cross had slipped down behind us into the world that was finally letting us go.

"The first conquerors in the north were the Vikings," Triebel said. "They landed on the North American coast long before other nations."

As we tried to trace Bartsch's home-made chart under the starry sky, without us noticing, the first officer came down from the chart room opposite and over to us. He enjoyed Bartsch's commentary and listened on with a smile. He spoke reasonable German and by following the drawing understood everything. Then he invited us to accompany him to the chart room, where every night the trainee officers verified the ship's course against the position of the stars. He asked Bartsch, who spoke Polish well, what our professions were. He said these professions appealed to him.

The first officer acknowledged that they would probably have performed the same task several hundred years ago. He said that nowadays they still needed to practice the art; although our ship was controlled automatically, the slightest interference in the signal and a cadet had to know how to produce the charts and pinpoint the ship's position against the stars, like in the old days.

The young men were far too engrossed to let us disturb them, far too tense as the first officer supervised one thing or another.

Compared with the rooms we passengers occupied, where constant noise and chatter dominated, here reigned unparalleled silence. Only a real idiot like Woytek, crashing about in my cabin, would have managed to shatter this studious silence—once a part of his job—with a mindless, raucous racket.

The officer told us he had only attended school until eighth grade. He first went to sea as a cabin boy. The sea had drawn him. Then he had spent his spare time on the ship preparing for his first exam and soon after that his next. One of the ship's mates was listening to him. He already had a seaman's face, composed, alert.

The following morning, Ernst Triebel told me:

"In Berlin I had to give a report, less about the exhibition as the matter of Dahlke. They were all set to severely reprimand me over Dahlke's disappearance, before my very eyes as it were, when Heinz Schulz (who had arranged for us to travel together) intervened. He was never lost for words, I noticed, even less so now than when we were in student halls. He didn't shy away from airing his views. Without formally asking to speak, he declared that not only I, Ernst Triebel, had got this damned Dahlke wrong, and furthermore, I couldn't possibly have kept him in line throughout the entire journey.

"Despite this, they didn't stop asking me preposterous questions such as: why did I not realize the man's intentions sooner, what did we speak about on the journey, with whom did Dahlke associate, and similar stuff. They also asked who recommended Dahlke for the trip and me in particular as his companion. When it transpired it was Dahlke's best friend, Professor Oehmke no less, some got suspicious. You saw that now they would also have doubts over Oehmke's trustworthiness. Luckily I kept my cool and my nerve during all these interviews. Only the people backed off from me again, as though I had newly arrived. They became strangers to me again, almost like a foreign people. When I was a student in student halls I found being here easier. You always had an inkling who had remained Nazi, who had put the Hitler era behind them for good, who was minded to start a new way of life. You kept much less hidden. You freely poured out your thoughts.

"One long, quite bizarre evening when everyone was puzzling over Oehmke (seeing as obviously we couldn't now change Dahlke's mind retrospectively), my friend Heinz Schulz lost his temper. He interjected angrily (however, what he shouted only served to prolong the so-called debate) then calmed down and sat quietly until the end. As we were both leaving together, out on the dark street he again lost his composure and said angrily: 'If I'd known you were coming back again and had no intention of staying over there, I wouldn't have got you the trip.'

"I said nothing to this remark; I found it offensive and hypocritical. So I wasn't particularly surprised either when, a year later, this Heinz Schulz flew with his Professor Oehmke from West Berlin to London and stayed there.

"Despite all the to-and-fro, during this time I finished my doctoral thesis. Now I was faced with the question where best I could further train in internal medicine. I looked for a post as an intern.

"I mention all these little details, trivialities, but you'll see that even these simple, self-evident things are leading me to one single point: to an encounter I had on the last evening I spent in the country we're now leaving. It was as though the country wouldn't let me go until my youth lit up again, lit up in a swirl of lights which then, after finally dispersing, left behind like ashes the question that even now I can't resolve.

"Although it would be a while before the Institute for Tropical Medicine opened in Rostock, there was still plenty of opportunity to study for myself. There was some research in Berlin and Leipzig, and sometimes they held courses there. But at the time I had no appetite for the big city. I told myself I still hardly knew the countryside, or as good as not at all. I didn't quite know how to combine my two desired courses of study, but instinctively I looked at posts offered in small towns, even villages in Thuringia and the Ore Mountains. I wrote to the hospital in Ilmenau where there was an intern position free. For some reason the name Ilmenau had stuck in my head. Only later did I remember that Maria Luisa once mentioned that she spent her childhood there until her mother's death. Then her father moved to Erfurt with his daughter and Aunt Elfriede, who no doubt was pretty then and of indispensable help. The company he worked for sent him to Brazil as a buyer. The country must have had a powerful effect on his imagination, his self-confidence, his spirit of enterprise. He accepted the offer that set him up there on his own two feet and resigned from his Erfurt job. Aunt Elfriede came over with little Maria Luisa. In Rio too she was virtually indispensable. She greatly boosted her brother-in-law, she spurred him on. Everything seemed to go well until suddenly the same thing befell him as did my cabin mate. He caught a bad fever. Perhaps he also drank and suffered sun stroke, a story the little girl needn't hear about…

"So Aunt Elfriede had to get by on her own with her niece.

"As soon as I had time off, I visited my father in Greifswald. I told him all my experiences: Maria's death, Dahlke's defection and my new posting. This time my father only listened distractedly.

"Suddenly he interrupted me and said: 'There's something you should know. I'm marrying again. The woman is kind and intelligent. Her husband died in the war. He must have been an upstanding man. She too was always upstanding and brave. In fact she was imprisoned for two years during the Hitler era.'

"Because I didn't comment right away, he added: 'You and I, we are and will remain the same friends.'

"'Of course,' I said. Though for no reason the thought went through my head: *that I don't yet know*. And because I wanted to say something nice I added: 'Now you won't need to sit around here anymore on your own every night.'

"'No, I won't need to anymore,' my father said. 'And she'll look after my friends, see to the flat. You'll meet her later, Ernst; she's coming to dinner.'

"I didn't say anything. I was silent. 'What are you thinking about?' my father asked.

"'Oh, something else entirely, Father. I don't know if you'll remember. One evening in Rio, we were sitting under the trees in the square in front of the post office. You had been telling me that my mother was dead and that now we'd move to the city, you and I. And while you explained this to me—this is what I was thinking about—a mulatto man sat down next to us. He played a tune on a strange instrument, ceaselessly yet softly. I now know the name of that instrument I saw and heard then for the first time: *berimbau*. Can you still remember the tune?'

"'Certainly not; I can't even remember the mulatto man.'

"I hummed him the tune as softly and steadily as the man had played it then. But my father said a second time: 'I don't know it anymore. Let's leave it.'

"I think that just as our silence began again the front doorbell rang downstairs. My father jumped up with a pleased look.

"I liked my father's fiancée more than I had imagined. You immediately spotted her nice quiet nature. Though not necessarily beautiful, she looked really good in her simple clothes.

"As I said goodbye I told my father this, and he was pleased and asked me to come and visit just as often as I could. *Probably I won't do that*, I thought again; *too much has changed for you and for me.*

"I took up my post in Ilmenau. When I arrived, I was pleased that my new hospital lay right at the forest's edge and was surrounded by different kinds of trees.

"My new boss was called Doctor Reinhard. He and I got on from day one. He suggested I stay at the house as they had a room spare for that purpose. I gladly took him up on the offer. We ate together, his friendly little wife and blonde daughter, tall like her father. They all listened eagerly to what I told them about my background, particularly my Brazilian boyhood. I also took the opportunity to ask if from time to time I could take one of the courses in tropical diseases that were held three or four times a year in several university towns. I said I would be happy to forego my holidays to attend. I showed them the few books I possessed. 'If only I understood more about it!' Reinhard exclaimed every so often. Or: 'If only I understood foreign languages like you! Portuguese, Spanish, English. Like you, I could really have got to grips with it there.'

"Erna, the daughter, was sorry her friend Herta wasn't there.

"'Herta has her head in the clouds as it is,' the doctor's wife said; 'she would have been awake all night after your stories.'

"The first thing I did in my time off was go to the cemetery. I found the grave of a lady by the name of Wiegand, who had likely been Maria Luisa's mother. I left some flowers.

"The very next day, the doctor asked me if one of my relatives was buried here. You saw how small the town was. 'No,' I said. But I felt good, almost like a Catholic, under the cover of this dead woman.

"The following evening, the friend by the name of Herta Gehring came round. She was a year younger than Erna, slender with black hair and gray-blue eyes. Again I had to show my books and photos. She listened enthralled, barely breathing. She asked if she could look at the photos in her spare time.

"Not long after that, I bumped into Herta on my way through the small town. We walked for a bit together. She asked me if it had not been hard to part from that wonderful country.

"'Very hard,' I replied. 'I could hardly get used to being here.'

"'Did you not leave anyone behind from your youth? Someone your whole heart was set on?'

"'And?'

"'Did you wait for her?'

"'I waited a long time for her; hoped she would come. Well, not that long ago she died.'

"'What did she die from?' Herta asked, and her curiosity contrasted strangely with her shyness.

"I hesitated with my reply: 'A lot of people there live next to the sea. They often go swimming and bathing; sometimes in their work break. She too lived by the beach. She drowned while swimming.'

"Herta thought long and hard. 'Who told you that?' The matter was apparently of such concern to her that she could hardly contain herself.

"'I was since there myself at a trade fair in São Paulo.'

"'Perhaps she died from missing you—when you've spent your entire youth with someone. I haven't known anything like that.'

"'Oh, you know what, Herta, she was actually married in the interim.'

"'What has that got to do with it? That way she can remain devoted to you. And while she was in the sea playing with her thoughts, she must have thought hard about you and in the process lost control.' We walked a long way together in silence.

"'What was her name?'

"'Maria Luisa.'

"'I don't think you'll ever forget her.'

"'Forget her? No. Never; she was my life. But all the same, some time has passed since then.'

"'What day did she die on?'

"'Oh, look Herta, I don't even know. I forgot to ask afterwards… Here we are at the hospital. Please come and have dinner with us this evening.'

"'My father is expecting me. I'll be along later for certain.'

"I went on numerous long walks with this girl. She knew her way around the forest and the hills, and only now did I see how soft and still the countryside can be in our native country. Herta was pleased when I said something like that. Yes, I associated the word 'stillness' with those same places we visited, with the deep forest and the hills. I associated the word 'stillness' with my native country. We also went to the places which became famous from Goethe staying there for whatever reason, a love affair or a hunting trip of his duke's. Goethe meant little to me. To me he comes across as pompous, always trying to be high-minded. It's as though he was fixated with posterity, while all the time his contemporaries had enough need of encouragement, living unheeded in miserable working conditions in the valleys. But I was afraid of mentioning any of this to Herta, which was far removed from all that he himself had wished to portray and really had left to posterity. I revealed nothing of these thoughts so as not to upset her because she had been brought up, both at home and at school, to see in Goethe a higher force of nature. Only with care could I cure her of that. We climbed the hill called the Kickelhahn and she showed me Goethe's famous poem, written by his hand, 'Over every Hill is Peace.' I noticed she carefully watched me to see if the poem produced the expected emotion. 'One of the loveliest nature poems I know in the German language,' I said, to which she asked what I meant by that, whether I could imagine anything more beautiful. 'Well then, Herta,' I replied, 'a nature poem, a poem which with eloquent words speaks not of nature, birds and trees but of human existence with all its joy and pain.'

"She asked me if I would translate a Spanish poem for her, for instance one by García Lorca, whom the fascists murdered. I had already told her about this.

"After a little thought, on the way home I translated the poem about the girl whose lover thinks her a virgin until she has removed all her many corsets and petticoats and lain down with him by the river as the 'distant dogs barked'.

"Even as I translated I sensed the poem was inappropriate, barely comprehensible to a young girl from Ilmenau.

"I also translated poems for her by Machado, who died in a concentration camp. His poems were more easily understandable to her. Then when we came to talking about bullfighting I tried to explain that it wasn't a barbaric duel with a defenseless animal, rather a symbol, the Spanish seeing a symbol of death in the dangerous proximity to the animal.

"I also told her about Mexico (a country I didn't know) and that there people painted more than wrote poetry. I promised to show her pictures of murals at home. I explained that the entire history of Mexico was painted in fresco on the wall of a loggia, open to the plain. Friends had told me that many an indigenous Mexican would tie their mule to a tree and go up to the loggia with wife and child and explain everything to them, from the evils of Cortez up to Zapata's white horse.

"Then we came to talk about the great Brazilian sculptor, Aleijadinho, and Herta asked me if I would show her the pictures again that evening.

"Out of nowhere she asked if I had seen Aleijadinho's statues with Maria Luisa. 'Yes,' I truthfully told her.

"Whereupon Herta said something striking: 'If I could see them with you I would be wholly changed. You will never forget Maria Luisa if you saw something together like that great stairway with the prophets.'

"I didn't know what to say. I remembered the hours Maria and I had spent in Belo Horizonte. My heart ached. How could I compare Herta's modest shyness to Maria Luisa's gleaming gold?

"At the same time I thought: *why should all girls gleam like gold? There are ungilded goddesses, white ones, other colors too…*

"A short time later, I received an unexpected invitation. I was quite unaware that I particularly stood out on the training courses I went to every two to three months; evidently my written work was better than many others'. And so when an invitation arrived to a conference on tropical medicine in Bahia, which would last about a month, they selected me.

"In the state of Bahia, especially in the main city of Salvador, there was far more research material than elsewhere, above all there were real-life cases. Added to which, I had never been in Bahia. I was surprised at suddenly being offered this opportunity, though truth be told I was no longer so desperate to see Brazil again. But seeing Bahia was important to me.

That part of the country had the most black inhabitants. Far more black than white. I gladly accepted the invitation.

My boss willingly gave me holiday leave. Only Herta was very concerned: 'Who knows if you'll come back again? That's the country of your youth, of your very being.'

"'What are you talking about?' I said, laughing. 'In the style of the classics... three quarters of people there are black. To me that's marvelous, but first and foremost completely alien. I want to see everything, learn all about it and then come back to Ilmenau. We haven't ever been to Erfurt, you and I. That's just as important to me now as Salvador.'

"But Herta stayed sad. Her little face trembled. She fought back tears. I was amazed how attached to me she was. At the same time I realized I had brought an entirely new, scintillating world of color into her life. It both troubled and pleased me.

"As a going-away present she gave me a posy of wild flowers (although she knew how quickly these would wither) and a dozen particularly nice apples, which would probably keep. She didn't know what to do when I fiercely kissed her. My present to her was a ring inset with small blue stones in the form of a forget-me-not. I couldn't remember buying it. I no longer knew where it came from. Maria Luisa definitely never wore jewelry like that. Maybe from my mother…?

"Herr Hammer, soon you'll see why we've found ourselves here on this self-same ship over a prolonged period, you and I. It so happens I've been able to tell you my whole life story, though admittedly my life is still relatively short. Short or long, I've told you the most important things. I myself am none the wiser for much of it."

"I think you've done well to tell me. You will feel a weight lifting."

"We're not finished yet. A bitter end is still to come."

Someone tapped me on the shoulder.

I turned round. Sadowski stood behind me. He laughed and said: "Come with me quickly to the crew area. I want to show you something."

As we climbed down, he continued: "The nun—I've already told you she has a soft spot for the crew—is sitting in Wladimir Klebs's cabin as we speak and he's serving her coffee and schnapps. It's a picture for the gods. She obviously doesn't think anybody's on the lookout for her, least of all in Wladimir's cabin. What's more, she's peering at him with eyes all rolling. Well, see for yourself."

We went past several doors before reaching Klebs's cabin. The sailor he shared with shooed us away. From time to time he came back with something to drink. Sadowski made various attempts to get the nun's attention, or to prevent Klebs offering her a fresh bottle.

Klebs was annoyed because he was being disturbed. He came out and asked for quiet so he could converse in peace. He said he had something of the utmost importance to discuss with the nun. By now I had realized that the two of them were having a conversation and that Sadowski's speculation was nonsense; Klebs's colleague wouldn't keep bringing coffee and cake into the cabin, unless there was a good reason to entertain the nun.

Eventually she left. The crew surrounded Wladimir Klebs and asked him the outcome of the conversation. Sadowski had already gone on his way, as though he sensed it was not for his ears. But the sailors were not shy to quiz Klebs. Klebs indicated to me that I was free to listen in.

Klebs told us the nun was an expert in writing for the blind, known as Braille. She had already taught Braille to dozens, even hundreds of blind children. The letters are vividly embossed onto the pages so that, with time, the child learning is able to feel the pages and thereby read. Little by little they can even decipher an atlas, but that's a difficult task which demands the child's concentration as well as that of the teacher, above all.

Now Wladimir Klebs had a little sister who years ago was blinded through illness. In Poland they were just in the process of establishing a lay school for the blind (at present there was a religious school for blind children, affiliated to a conventional religious school). By chance Klebs had bumped into this nun once before. She had urged him to send his little sister to her school. She said the lay school might not open for years; why should the child have to wait so long?

Klebs told us the nun was even trying to introduce the Braille system in Brazil. A group of nuns were busy there now, transposing Braille script into Portuguese. She hoped to have a big influx into her own schools as a result. But Klebs told us that his family, unlike many Polish families, was strongly opposed to the church. They were resisting sending the child to such a school.

Klebs had told the nun all this. She insisted his main objective should still be to have the child educated at a good school, so she could have a reasonably normal life. But Klebs knew that if he suggested this, his father would only get angry. What did she mean by a reasonably normal life? The child will swap one deficiency for another. The big question is which deficiency is the more serious. The nun said that, if faced with a similar question, she would have to say: the spiritual.

We spent half the night discussing the nun's offer and the pros and cons for Klebs's little sister.

We urged Klebs first and foremost to track down a teacher at the proposed lay school and ask their advice. He also needed to know when this new lay school was expected to open. If imminently, then the whole issue was resolved. Strangely, Klebs was hesitant, as though he was already indebted to the nun for all her help and encouragement. Perhaps he himself would have preferred to send the child straight to the religious school.

*W*hen I was alone again with Triebel I asked him to tell me all about Bahia because I too had never been there. I think I already mentioned that I prefer travelers' tales to love stories.

So Triebel began again: "We flew by plane to Salvador. On the way back I intended to go by boat because I had to transport a veritable library of books, which I had been instructed to buy back home. You must remember that during the war a vast amount of material was burnt. My cargo would make a plane journey excessively expensive.

"At the airport I was met by representatives of the conference, all black people of smart and cheerful disposition. They took me to a small hotel. The conference didn't have much money at its disposal, added to which not a great many participants had come: a few French, two Swedish, a Soviet professor, various Latin Americans and one unprejudiced North American.

"I was soon used to seeing far more black people than white around me. I don't know how they regarded us. They probably couldn't have cared less what color our skin was. I was amazed how many churches there were. I saw a good many black people knelt in prayer, primarily women.

"'Usually they go to church either from superstition, remembrance, or feelings of exuberance,' my companion said, a young doctor by the name of Da Castro.

"After a while, I noticed an amulet on his neck and asked him why he wore it. 'That's not an amulet,' he unashamedly told me; 'it's a sign; it informs our friends that I belong to a very specific group, the elders that take our group's services. Have you never heard of Candomblé, then?'

"'I only know the Macumba sect from Rio,' I said guardedly, 'Now and then you find little piles of ashes, like after a small fire, where they hold their ceremonies, or else to ward off malicious neighbors. They hold a big celebration annually on the beach for a sea goddess, with song and dance. Is a festival like that meant to be a pagan or a religious practice?'

"Da Castro became angry: 'Why are you worried whether such a practice is purportedly pagan or religious? How do you differentiate the two? How do you tell the pagan is pagan? Or the religious religious, except by the priests' pious talk? And you can't even rely on that.'

"'But somehow they trace back to reason. Perhaps in a

circuitous way. Perhaps they are derived from old ways. But not only in the worship of nature.'

"'Come one evening and see everything yourself,' Da Castro interrupted. 'We only have seminars in the afternoons.'

"I must add that I was surprised by the standard of the medical seminars; there was no hint whatsoever of any malpractice. They were also very willing to help me select reading material for home. Da Castro was a doctor at a leprosy clinic. His explanations, always strictly scientific, had nothing to do with the strange allusions he sometimes dared make in our conversations alone. Only once, when I asked him if any of his patients also wore an amulet (he had explained that they gave the wearer the right to belong to a particular higher circle), he briskly replied: 'Of course; why not?'

"We studied day and night with the locals' help. How I would have liked to stay there, to be able to continue my studies. For a short period my life in Ilmenau became a thing of the past. I even stopped thinking about little gray-eyed Herta. White skin soon became alien to me. But I sensed my state would only last for as long as I stayed here.

"Da Castro openly told me the difficulties he had overcome in order to attend high school, and even more so when it came to university. They had no money for books, not even old ones, so they borrowed them individually for hours at a time from the library. And his ambitious mother supported her son with all manner of work from home. When he successfully passed his exams they gave a party the likes of which he would never experience again.

"The examination and treatment of patients in Da Castro's

hospital stood somewhat in contrast to encounters with lepers on the street. Their situation appeared quite hopeless. They probably just earned a living by begging. Mostly they stayed with their families. No one paid them particular regard. They were a part of life on the street and even a doctor only discovered one here and there in the crowd if they really looked.

"Understandably, I saw not one white person in the Candomblé tent, wide as a house, that Da Castro took me along to that evening. The women's robes swayed to the sound of passionate singing. They occupied one half of the tent, the men stood in the other. And the leader for the evening the chairwoman, the priestess—was a big dignified lady with men and women before her where she sat, amidst the tremendous tumult in the tent. Around her stood some male elders, including Da Castro, identifiable by their various amulets announcing their affiliation. I compared Da Castro's mindset during the congregation's singing and dancing with his attentiveness during our seminars. Perhaps as a boy he had been put off the customs of a cloister and come to a kind of natural religion.

"From Africa the black people brought their customs which sustained them despite slave ships, despite chains. There was no more slavery here now. But black people were still united by their ancient traditions.

"As a boy I had occasionally attended one of those Macumba gatherings. Here I was witnessing pure paganism for the first time in my life, not in the least barbaric, rather with many set conventions which, like the women's costumes, I imagined must stem from the slavery era, when it signified a step towards freedom for these people's forebears to meet together somewhere secretly at night with dancing and singing, summoned by the drums' dull thudding that only they understood. White people in Africa today still fear the call of the primeval drum. But black people here were free. Their celebration was an imitation of ancient customs.

"The people taking part in the ceremony believed the gods they invoked, rather than speak to them, conjoined with them in order to speak *from* them, from within, from inside their soul as it were. The moment they felt the deity enter, they fell to the floor with emotion and writhed in ecstasy.

"Da Castro was disappointed because the ceremony didn't make the impression on me he had hoped. I tried explaining to him that, from my understanding, the people gathered together from ancient tradition. He was just annoyed by my reasoning. He asked me if I wished to speak alone with the priestess to seek clarification or to ask her for advice. But I replied that, no, I had no need whatsoever to take advice from priests or the clergy. Da Castro regretted that my life was a pretty poor one. 'It may be,' I replied, 'my life could be freer, richer and happier were I to adhere to various customs like you.'

"I used the time I had while still in Bahia to see as much as possible, but above all to make useful purchases for our libraries. By the end I had amassed such sizeable parcels that a journey by boat was essential. To my joy, the Polish ship I most wanted to sail home on was sitting in Bahia at the time—the *Norwid*, which we're on now. It was due to sail in two days' time and would make a stop in Ilhéus, where a considerable quantity of cocoa was expected. I deposited my parcels on board and greeted the captain and his officers. We were only a few passengers. Most would come from Rio, for instance you, the singer who had been on tour, his wife, the consul's wife and her children, our star expert friend Bartsch (his aunt always hoped he would stay with her in Belo Horizonte, but he wanted to get back to his mine), Woytek, your current cabin mate (as I have it, he had to get his travel documents from the embassy in Rio and in addition ask for his fare), and a few others who boarded later. From the outset, the nun was with us on board with her thin travel companion. Both had come from a cloister in Bahia. She already sat at a separate little table then and spoke only with her companion, who also seemed nun-like to me.

"I invited Da Castro aboard. I drank Wiśniówka with him and showed him round our entire ship. As you know, she's almost new. He expressed his admiration, but he was no longer as open and friendly as when I first arrived. I think my reservations about his meetings had deeply hurt him, as though thereby I had mocked a believer's religion.

"Despite this, he guided me round and showed me lots of places. We went to many restaurants where there was not only food and drink, but music and dance. He also took me to hidden harbor areas—how easy it was to slip past the security and customs officials—to cellar-dwellings where his friends and sometimes even patients stayed, happily living away in cramped, gloomy conditions. It was as though the dankness in the cellar was on the point of breaking free from its claustrophobic humid underground environment to mingle with the indescribably sweet, enticing sound of guitars and song.

"He showed me the main market. I was quite overcome by the smell of fruit, all the fruits of the country. I was hypnotized by the jewelry, many kinds of necklaces of strung seeds from fruit I had never seen before here in the Brazilian countryside. Some seeds were hairy but fiery-red inside, others smooth as a girl's skin but pale green. And they said that this necklace was for a mulatto girl, that one for a white girl and various other ones were for black girls. Had I stayed there longer I might have better understood the people's beliefs, Da Castro's beliefs too.

"Many of the stalls brimmed with every type of trinket, pendants of pretty pearls that looked like berries on a bush. And there were also real bushes, and some fruit stalls sold bananas and other fruit that normally grow on palms but which here grew in passages between the stalls.

"Suddenly I thought to buy every kind of fruit to take to Herta, one of each, unripe and carefully wrapped (as they would have plenty of time to ripen on the way). She was fascinated by such fruit. Suddenly feeling myself alone, I bought little presents for the doctor's daughter and my father's wife. One got a colorful bracelet, the other a fish-shaped comb.

"There were stalls selling sundry items of really shabby clothing. No doubt cellar-dwellers like the ones we visited stocked up here. There was also a hall full of leather goods with skillfully carved items on display. I bought myself a sturdy pair of sandals made of hide for the winter.

"On our last evening in Bahia they gave us a party of sorts. Our host hadn't attended the conference; he was a member of an academy, a doctor known throughout the country. He was friendly with one of the delegates and was aware that we didn't have much money left for festivities. The women of the family prepared all the food. There was plenty of drinking. The occasional guest also ate and drank with us, some perhaps patients of his, appeasing hunger and thirst and enjoying making merry. Many got just one glass of wine and a plateful of fruit.

"We all sat mixed together with no seating arrangement in a big wood-paneled room. There were windows in every wall so that from wherever you sat you saw the sea, because this house where we were guests on that last evening was on a headland. The terraces and gardens took it up entirely.

"Our host told us that the previous week a sick man was rowed ashore to the house from a passing ship. Such incidents were commonplace, he told us. This sick man, a black sailor, had come down with a bad fever whilst on board and suffered another seizure shortly before reaching dry land. In the ensuing panic even he, the doctor, hadn't immediately been able to ascertain the cause of illness. They merely notified the sick man's family, who lived here. It remained unclear what would happen with the man.

"A doctor who had attended our conference offered to take the sailor to his hospital after a certain time, if meanwhile our host was prepared to look after him in his own house.

"The whole arrangement struck me as complicated, practically unfeasible, but he animated our guests, evidently offering them more a form of entertainment. While we talked you heard wave after wave hit the garden terraces. Depending on which window you happened to look out of, now you saw a rowing boat close in laden with vegetables on the way to market, now a motor boat far off following the coast at a certain distance.

"Two boys, white, not black, came bursting in bearing baskets laden with all manner of fruit. They set down their baskets and gave us a remarkably accomplished acrobatic display. We learned that these blonde acrobats were the doctor's sons.

"The constant view of the ocean with all its boats, the cry of the birds, the rhythm of the waves, and the whole care-free atmosphere of the guests gave me the feeling I was already sailing on a ship.

"We carried on drinking and singing so long that in the end I went straight aboard my ship in the early hours, after fetching my hand luggage. We lay close to shore. Along the coast stood church after church, partly obscured by dust-laden palm trees. The purser inspected my travel papers. Da Castro came aboard one last time to wish me a good journey. He was astonished at the nun and her quite substantial entourage, as all sorts of people—friends, lay sisters and nuns—had accompanied her aboard to say goodbye.

"A small thin couple who spoke Portuguese sat at my table. Lots of black people, probably farm laborers, lay around on deck or ran between cargo holds.

"Because in Bahia we were missing everyone who would board in Rio, we were only a few beginning our journey to Europe here.

"In Ilhéus the thin couple left us. Perhaps they were merchants. The ship anchored offshore because there was no proper harbor. I was very impressed by the couple's agility as they jumped from the ship's steps into the small motor launch, which then took them to shore. Evidently they were used to the journey. I noted how many black people likewise left the ship out here on open water, perhaps having committed to work on cocoa plantations in Bahia. The boats the black people rowed from shore were filled to the gunnels with cocoa sacks.

"It took a good full day until our cocoa was loaded. The sacks were lowered into the cargo hold under the ganger's orders. I counted up how many sacks of cocoa Berlin needed for one winter. At intervals the black men rowed back to shore to reload their boats. I listened to their singing, which sounded tired and restrained. Only occasionally did a voice rise up, one single voice, in joyous abandon. For all the sacks of cocoa they brought aboard our little Polish ship, the work scarcely merited the genuine joy of a song. Do these people have a labor union? How much do they get paid per day? Perhaps by the man who climbed from the ship earlier? *Their wage will be a fraction of a song, tinged with melancholy*, and I thought too: *they are made to take on the work for all who know an easier life*.

"Finally as night fell the last boats were rowed home. At a distance you made out the palm fronds of the forest. The lonely lights of farms and villages shone over to our ship. We set sail.

"Along the way they informed us that the *Norwid* wouldn't sail to Rio but straight to Santos. We still had coffee to load there. The Rio passengers would all go to Santos and board there.

"For some reason the purser decided he needed to check over my registration documents, so again I had to stand in the queue of boarding passengers. You will recall, Hammer, that you were behind me."

"Yes," I said. "I also heard that you were German and would disembark in Rostock. The drunk Pole was already lying in the cabin I was allocated. He had wrecked the place. I went straight back out to wash and asked the ship's mate to sort things out."

"This incident," Triebel said, "you never mentioned it before."

"Because it's unimportant. You, Triebel, seemed full of the joys at the departure, that is, the sea journey you had ahead. At least that was the impression I got that day. I was quietly wondering when I would finally be with my family again. You, though, were telling me how you knew the ship's cook, that he must have purchased all kinds of fruit at the markets last thing. All the same I think it was then, on our first day, that you began telling me about the first time you went to Brazil and the adversities you had to face there as a schoolboy. Then the girl helped you with learning the language."

"Well, Hammer, yes, that's how it began. But now I need to tell you something else that happened on my last night in Santos. Do you mind?"

"How could I? I'm glad if you trust me. It's only now on this journey that I actually realize how rare it is that someone really trusts me, and I them. I don't know why that is—my own reserve, or a feeling that's gradually taken root that trusting others too much means to a certain extent giving yourself away, betraying all your private thoughts and feelings. God knows what may come of that. Of course, that's not a very good attitude for a human being.

"So I'm grateful to you for speaking so openly with me. At

first I was taken aback. Now it's doing me good."

"What I'm going to tell you now, though, this is not good.

"Did I already tell you that in Bahia they suddenly informed us we would go via Ilhéus and then to Santos, rather than to Rio? The other passengers would come by plane or train from Rio to São Paulo, and then from there down to Santos, to our ship. The change was because we had to load coffee in Santos.

"It was all the same to me. There was nothing especially binding me to Rio.

"When we arrived in Santos I wandered around the streets for an hour. Everywhere you looked coffee sacks were being filled and loaded. The ground crunched underfoot from coffee beans.

"I inquired after a good hotel because it would be next day at the earliest that we sailed. I was promptly recommended the Excelsior Hotel.

"With its many annexes the Excelsior Hotel was something like a castle. It gleamed with decaying splendor, crystal chandeliers and gilded fittings. An unpleasant odor lingered in the corridors, from as far back as imperial times, I think.

"Since I only had to stay that night and would be on board the very next day, in God's name I took one of these lavish stuffy rooms.

"As I walked through the foyer, in the strange half-light of the flickering crystal chandeliers and the remaining daylight I saw at a big round table a party of ladies young and old, laden with jewelry. They were immersed in a card game. The young ones were flushed from excitement, the older ones sallow. Some had dyed hair, others fresh and fragrant. All, however, were passionately immersed in the game.

"After I had washed and shaved in my room and put on a fresh shirt (which took all of twenty minutes), I went through this same foyer again to get something to eat.

"The half-light was gone. Every last crystal chandelier was ablaze. The ladies young and old were still seated round the table. It was obvious from their behavior that the game would soon reach its climax.

"I wanted to get out of there fast. Through a window I saw a few tables set in the garden. On the threshold I ran into a tall, immaculately dressed man of about my age. We both stopped in our tracks. The other man took me by the shoulders and cried: 'Ernesto, it's you! Are you here on a flying visit or have you actually been staying here?'

"Rodolfo seemed hardly to have changed from our schooldays: the smooth face with brilliant, smiling teeth. 'I was at a conference,' I replied. 'My ship, a Polish ship, leaves in the early hours.'

"'Then we must have a cognac together,' Rodolfo said. 'Wait; I'll get my wife. She's one of the witches at the card table.'

"The card player he approached reluctantly came over. 'My child, at least say hello to him.'

"She smiled with only the corners of her mouth. As though by chance, pinned in her rich brown hair was a solitary large comb glittering with pearls. The dress that smoothly hugged her tall slender figure, her upright posture, was white like her skin. I froze; Maria Luisa was standing before me. She kept her eyes sternly, if not fiercely fixed on the middle of my face, as though telling me to keep quiet at all costs.

"'He travels back in the early hours,' Rodolfo said, 'so I thought we could sit down together for a little.'

"His wife turned her face to him: 'I'm sorry. We're right at the all-exciting point in our game.'

"When I saw her profile and heard the sound of her voice, I was no longer so sure this lady could be Maria Luisa. Perhaps Rodolfo had found a second wife who was similar to his first wife, the dead one. 'Then we'll sit at your table and look on for a little,' he said.

"'Impossible,' his wife said in a somewhat childish, somewhat timid voice that couldn't belong to any dead person I knew, rather an unknown living one. 'That, as they say, would bring us bad luck.'

"'Every evening these crazy women are inseparable from their cards,' Rodolfo said, laughing.

"'He exaggerates,' his wife said; 'don't believe a word he says'. And now, as she turned her face to me again and this time spoke softly yet decisively, I was overcome anew by an unbearable aching, a terrible tormenting doubt: *are you Maria Luisa?* 'I must be away as early as possible,' I said, 'so all the best to you both.'

"Rodolfo said he regretted the hasty goodbye. He had hoped we would have a cognac and, when the game was finished—because surely it had to end some time—have dinner together.

"We shook hands. The lady who was or wasn't Maria Luisa gave me another fixed look—with all the pain this difficult goodbye was causing her, I thought.

"I swiftly changed my plans. I went back to my stuffy room. I threw myself onto the bed and lay there for a few hours. Two thoughts raced round and round in my head: *it was her—it wasn't her*.

"Can a person change so much that they are glued to a card table after our glorious youth? They can. Why not? They can completely change in Rodolfo's company. *Then there's no reason to mourn her loss. Forget her.* How am I supposed to forget my dead Maria Luisa? It wasn't her at all. When this lady bowed her head under that great comb, she was a stranger to me.

"Besides, the last time I came to this country Emma had been there to describe to me exactly how she drowned, through my fault as it were, after long futile waiting. Cold-hearted Eliza had laughed at such conjecture—even if she did confirm her death. Eliza claimed Maria Luisa grew to be happy with Rodolfo. She lost her life in an accident. But she had enjoyed it until the final hour.

"If that's true, then it may also easily be true that she had completely changed. Then the worst case scenario is possible. Then it may also be possible that Rodolfo—with whom she was happy—sent Emma to the terminal to convince me Maria Luisa was dead; so I didn't bother them again in their contented existence. Her friend Eliza—who without music was cold as ice—likewise lied to me. Because somehow they thought there remained a hint of danger in Maria's last paper-thin memory of our shared youth. Yes, rather all this agony than any hint of that danger.

"Did Maria know anything of the deception? Maybe even collaborate? That too is possible. Just an element of the shocking, soul-shattering sea change she suffered. Perhaps they simply kept my arrival from her, even though I was on the list of invitees to the trade fair in São Paulo. Because they thought she couldn't cope with seeing me again. Not yet cope—because now, tonight, she's coped.

"No, this lady tonight bears no resemblance, hardly any, to the real Maria Luisa. Why then this compulsion to do her such terrible injustice? It isn't Rodolfo I'm jealous of, it's death. Whether she slipped on rocks or was caught in a current, intentionally or unintentionally—what do I know. Neither is it my job to spend eternity investigating. Death seized her there in the sea and, before sweeping her away, it tossed her thin white body several times against the rocks—out of jealousy, because she was as beautiful as *Yemanjá*, the sea goddess, who alone may dare play with death at that spot.

"On a table in the hall, head slumped, a congealed trickle of blood at the corner of her mouth, broken limbs lifeless, that was how she lay in the end, the dead Maria Luisa. So Emma described it. And the people came crowding in to see the wondrous dead lady, and powerless death ground its terrible teeth afresh, again out of jealousy.

"No, the woman with the glittering comb in the hotel foyer was a stranger.

"But what if it was her after all? What if she *had* put that comb in her hair? Emma may have lied to me; Emma always was loyal to her employers. To say nothing of Eliza—to her lying is a veritable treat.

"Rodolfo may also have found out that we had written each other love letters again. And in accordance with his character and the laws of the country, she could never have come to me. Nor marry a second time. Now forced to stay with him and in his circle of friends, she may have thought: *there's nothing else for it*. And she gives up everything, any memory of our happy life. She loses herself in the gaudy mire, has her hair done and dresses up so that he can be proud of her...

"No, no. I do my Maria Luisa a terrible injustice, an injustice I myself will suffer from forever. Sooner or later, a wealthy man like Rodolfo finds the woman with the face and body of his dead beloved. He finds her because he never really actually loved the first one, the dead one; he played a little love game. It was *I* who loved her, which is why she cannot be dead to me. I can imagine it for a moment at most. Then I need only think of our youth together, so vivid and real. Nor do I wish to think of anything else any more. I want no more...

"How long have we been on this ship for now, Hammer? How long is it since I ran into Rodolfo in the Excelsior Hotel and saw the lady who was as alike as two peas to my Maria Luisa? Maybe she *was* Maria Luisa? Maybe it really was her after all—only horribly changed? Not changed at all, and changed horribly. In that shameful setting she had fallen into. Because nothing is impossible, Hammer, anything, *anything* is possible—any kind of change, however great, for better, for worse. But yet, no. That's not true."

Now I was worked up myself. "Precisely!" I exclaimed. "It's not true. And if you know that yourself, Triebel, then why do you keep going over the same old story?"

Triebel continued in a changed tone, as though he now had to reassure me: "Sometimes you hear of these kinds of dubious dodgy dealings. But inside a person there has to be an indestructible core, albeit sometimes hidden in the haze or lost in the mire, which even so lights up again in its original splendor. There *has* to be. I myself detected it in the last letter Maria Luisa wrote to me. Why am I beginning to doubt it anew here on the ship? Surely it's a sin to doubt Maria Luisa? She is dead, end of story. And no one can bring her back to life. Why this compulsion to portray her as leading some sort of unresolved double life?"

"We've been underway for eighteen days now," I said. "Please, Ernst Triebel, stop torturing yourself with this thing once and for all. Let your Maria Luisa be dead. Under no circumstances will you see the woman again. I implore you: put an end to all this senseless torment."

Triebel was quiet for a time. Then he said: "It's turned a lot cooler. It's a long time since we saw any flying fish. Tonight, Bartsch will show us that the Southern Cross has finally slipped away into southern eternity and the Great Bear arisen in our own sky."

"I really would like to study the sky with you both tonight," I said. "But only today the captain invited us to drink a Slivovitz, maybe for the last time. And do you know what the little cook promised? Exactly what you predicted on the first day: he's baking apples for us all; because he fetched them for the journey home."

"It's such a good smell. I already look forward to it," Ernst Triebel said. "We'll go up with Bartsch after we've had our apples."

𝒜t the meal, I told Sadowski what I had learnt from Klebs about the nun. He gave me a wary look.

"You don't have children, then?" I asked.

"What would you know about it?" he replied brusquely. "Maybe I've left behind a pretty Pole in Argentina, with a little girl."

After our Slivovitz, I stood under the steps again with Triebel. Just as he was about to begin again, I interrupted: "I don't want to hear any more of your worries and woes. Did you not say you're a doctor? Are you going to break into despair every time a patient is in danger?"

"I cannot believe you're telling the truth, Hammer," Triebel said. "You're just trying to pacify me now. You would have me believe it doesn't matter whether Maria has deceived me or not. Things are not that simple. In Ilmenau I'll discover if she's written to me. If she loves me without fear of the consequences, then I'll urge her to come to Rostock at once."

"My dear Triebel, she will not come; she is dead."

"That is the question, which remains unresolved. I cannot believe in her death."

For a long time Triebel said nothing.

"We could do with Bartsch now to have him explain the northern night sky," I said at last. "But he's playing chess with the Polish boy."

We retired to our cabins. I was surprised the man sharing mine wasn't there. Because I didn't feel like sleeping, I went on deck again. As I went up the steps, I noticed the captain arm in arm with Woytek, walking up and down on deck as Triebel and I had grown used to.

Later, Woytek came to the cabin. He was restless for a time, but did get to sleep quicker than usual. The captain had probably pacified him and given him some ideas for the future.

We might both have enjoyed a decent night's sleep, but there was a loud knock at the door. Outside were Triebel and Bartsch. They had come to fetch us because you could see the beacon near Brittany, what they call the first light of Europe. We rushed up, even though only a pinprick of light shone from the beacon. But all the same I know that we were all filled with a deep surging joy upon seeing the lighthouse at Brittany. We couldn't quite say why this first light of Europe suddenly filled us all with such satisfaction.

Speaking only for myself, it was fairly evident: very soon I would see my two children and my wife again, and my place of work. Despite the bother my last-minute departure caused me, I could now tell them what an incredulous welcome I was given in Rio Grande do Sul because of our lightning-fast response to our client's call. Above all, I looked forward to seeing my two girls again. They had plaits with ribbons in. How funny it will be to hear their chitter-chatter, half like frogs, half like birds.

Woytek must have been thinking about his conversation with the captain. For him too it was good to be going back. The captain had promised him a temporary position in Gydnia and advised he take a course in seamanship at the same time, ideally the same one he had passed previously (then he needn't fear bad luck in the exam). Once he passed, he would soon find a suitable job and none of his former colleagues or relatives need be aware of where he had hung out in the interim. Woytek was fully in agreement with this suggestion. Apparently he had tormented himself with the idea during his bad spell.

As ever, you saw from the captain's behaviour that he was the right man for our ship. I also liked the fact that he did his own washing on deck in the communal washing machine, and hung it all up. The crew must also have noticed this, though they said nothing. The nun silently let her skinny assistant take care of her washing. The captain was a strong, strong man. Admittedly the nun wasn't thin and emaciated herself.

We all had the feeling we were heading for the light the whole time, but it was an illusion. Instead we were heading away, towards the entrance to the English Channel. Soon the lighthouse would be redundant in the daylight. The first officer, who was watching this first light of Europe as intently as us, suddenly said: "The lighthouse stands on the island of Ushant, at the entrance to the English Channel. There is any amount of rocks around the island which are dangerous to small craft, particularly fishing boats, so a proverb has arisen." He told us the proverb in French: "*Qui voit Quessant, voit son sang*", and we all gathered round to hear the Polish and German translations: whoever sees Ushant sees their blood.

"Nothing will happen to us here," Bartsch said; "if we had sailed a little later in the year we would have run into the equinox. Then our journey might have been rougher."

"It really would be a terrible coincidence if I was invited to Brazil again," Triebel said. "I cannot ever see that part of the world again now."

"You would never see Maria Luisa again in any case," I said sternly. "Let the dead bury the dead."

However, he said: "And what if I find a letter when I get back?"

"Then burn it."

Meanwhile, the nun and her helper, and the singer and his wife had come over to us. The nun regarded the lighthouse with admiration. She called out a few phrases in Polish, perhaps even Latin, which her companions repeated word for word. Probably all of them together were thanking God for their arrival.

"Excellent!" Bartsch said. "We've made the journey in the shortest time possible. Without deviation."

"It felt a good old way to me at least," Woytek said gruffly, as he had muttered everything to himself during these days.

In the hours that followed, various types of tankers and freighters and all sorts of ships of varying sizes came from all sides. You sensed an impetus towards the English Channel.

"If you really go to sea," the little Polish girl suddenly said to her brother, "then you'll be an engineer like our dad."

"No I won't," the boy said stubbornly. "I intend to do something special."

Before his parents could ask him what that something special was, the captain said: "We'll try you out and see what you're good at."

A ship flying the Polish flag sailed very close and people onboard shouted over to us. I think their words were some kind of blessing along the lines of: thanks be for our arrival and we also give thanks for the lighthouse we see before us now.

Turning round suddenly, Bartsch said: "We give thanks to you, Herr Captain, and your entire crew."

At last, Triebel had been quiet. Suddenly he softly said what was on his mind, nevertheless: "And if she left the country long before us?"

"Stop this once and for all," I snapped fiercely. "She is dead. End of story. Yes, she drowned at sea, as you described to me. Now grant her what we call eternal rest. I am asking you nicely: do not speak of her again."

The first officer was watching us. I saw that he easily guessed the plot to such stories; he must hear them often on his travels.

The day we sailed through the Channel was sunny and clear. It was late summer. The sunlight, unimpeded by storms at this time of year, glowed gently on the opposite coast. And even with the many ships intersecting, this coast looked incredibly near. We stared at the multi-storied warehouses, office buildings and various apartments. In the clear, soft dissipating light we even made out the individual floors with their verandas, where people were lying or exchanging news or going about their business.

The coast seemed to come to us. It seemed much higher and steeper than it actually was.

"What a wonderful island!" Bartsch shouted. You see, we had no idea we were only seeing a promontory. Had we been able to take a train we would soon have traveled over level ground.

Again Sadowski quizzed us about what we had read of Joseph Conrad. Now above all he wanted to know if we remembered the description of when the Romans seized this mighty island and overcame a coastline such as this.

"In Conrad's book, the people discuss this on a boat sailing down the Thames in the present day," Sadowski added, "and they are amazed by how savage the world once was here too."

I was deeply impressed that a man like Sadowski had read so much, and at the same time I felt envy because as boys we had helped my father in the fields, at most played a little football and hardly ever read. But this Sadowski was obviously well-versed on many areas.

However, Bartsch retorted angrily: "How about the Germans firing on the English occupation of Dunkirk. And entire areas of London burning down in air attacks? Has the world not remained savage?"

Meanwhile, the Channel had widened out. We saw into the mouth of the Elbe. We all rushed over from the Channel side to the mainland side of the ship. Lots of different ships were surging deeper and deeper into the mainland and just as many ships from Hamburg had started to navigate their way out to sea.

We docked at the port of Brunsbüttel. The purser came round each one of us with his list. During the short stop you could buy what you wanted, duty-free. I chose colorful little knitted jackets for my wife and daughters.

Triebel sat on his own, withdrawn even from his friends. He had his arms crossed on the railing and his head resting on his hands. He looked out over the plain we were sailing through. It was an unfamiliar sight. I don't know if he had made this journey before by ship through green farmland, and it was indeed strange to be plowing through fields of corn instead of big waves out on the lonely ocean.

What Triebel said about his childhood is true. There was not a word of a lie to it. Without doubt his account was pure, unadulterated truth. I fear he will not get over this sorrow so easily. Nothing is harder to overcome than the pain and suffering you went through when you were young. You can never forget it. Generally we claim the opposite. We say the pain from our younger years is easy to forget. I don't believe that. I too will never forget the difficult things I experienced in my youth: my favorite brother's death, and my best friend's lingering death as he lay helpless on the open field. How do you get over a sorrow like Triebel's? It weighs on your soul forever, and perhaps you will be angry with me because I believe that also has its good side. In this ever changing, ever aspiring world we live in today, it's good if something permanent stays preserved in you forever, even if that permanence is a sorrow you cannot forget. Because he has experienced something difficult he will understand all those who have been through something difficult. And this "understanding others" will serve him his entire life, and in his work too.

The autumn afternoon wore on with its pale frugal light. A thin, intangible shadow settled in front of me. Someone put their arm around my shoulder. I knew instantly it had to be Triebel, surrendering his solitude.

"I'm glad I've told you everything that happened to me, Hammer," he said; "I feel a weight has lifted, as though I've thrown one stone after the other into the sea. Now I look forward to being home—I mean, it isn't really home yet, but it shall be—to the little town of Ilmenau and the hospital there, and my work caring for my patients, and reporting on the Bahia conference, and delivering the books I purchased. I even look forward to seeing my head doctor and his family, and quiet little gray-eyed Herta. How good that I've brought each a separate little present in my suitcase. It's even possible, Hammer, that Herta will meet me in Rostock."

"Everything that you have told me has greatly enriched my journey," I said. "You shouldn't now build up your hopes too high that this Herta will come and meet you in Rostock. It's a long way from Thuringia to the Baltic Sea."

"She sort of hinted at it in a letter," said Triebel, "otherwise the idea wouldn't have entered my head. I'd be pleased, but I don't necessarily expect her…"

Meanwhile, it had gone completely dark. We ate our evening meal slowly and subdued. No one felt like having a drink or raising a glass. All of us went early to bed.

When we got up a few hours later, Triebel was already sitting in his old spot. He was chatting with Bartsch. Here and there among the branches you saw one or two apples, golden and red golden, shining like little suns.

Biographical Note
Douglas Irving

Crossing contains many biographical threads from Anna Seghers's own life experience. In particular, during her lifetime she made three return Atlantic crossings: in 1941 she sailed from France to Mexico, and then back to Europe in 1947; in the 1960s she twice sailed from the German Democratic Republic (GDR) to Brazil and back.

As a leftist, antifascist writer, Anna Seghers had to flee Nazi Germany in 1933 along with her husband, the Marxist economist László Radványi and their two young children, Ruth and Peter. The Jewish family found sanctuary in France, near Paris, until Nazi troops advanced on Paris in 1940. Forced deeper into exile from Hitler, the family fled over the Pyrenees to Marseilles and in 1941 found a passage aboard a cargo steamer across the Atlantic to Martinique.

After months of detour and delay, including an unsuccessful attempt to enter North America, the family reached Mexico. Here Anna Seghers remained in exile until 1947 when she sailed back across the Atlantic to Sweden. She then traveled onwards to France, to where Peter and Ruth had been sent in 1945 and 1946. She continued to Germany without her children and husband, as László Radványi had stayed in Mexico to teach at university there. He would return in 1952.

After 14 years in exile, Anna Seghers returned to a devastated and disorienting Berlin (see "The Visit" excerpt, below). She was now the internationally bestselling author of the classic work of exile literature, *The Seventh Cross* (1942). She eventually settled in East Berlin, in what would become the GDR. The emerging socialist nation bestowed her with honor. She was a central figure of GDR literary and cultural life, attending the 1949 Paris World Peace Congress and that of Warsaw in 1950, where she became a member of the World Peace Council. On page 94 of *Crossing* Ernst Triebel mentions the Stockholm Appeal, the 1950 worldwide accord for a universal ban on nuclear weapons. Anna Seghers was a signatory along with many intellectuals, scientists, artists and writers including Dmitri Shostakovich, Pablo Picasso, Pablo Neruda and Jorge Amado.

The Brazilian writer Jorge Amado became a lifelong friend to Anna Seghers, and invited her to Brazil in 1961. She and her husband set off from East Berlin, via Warsaw, to Gdynia on the Baltic coast, from where they sailed to Rio. On the return leg, aboard a Polish cargo ship carrying coffee, they visited the coastal cities of Salvador da Bahia and Ilhéus, Amado's childhood home. In 1963 Seghers visited Amado a second time. She was mainly in Salvador, where she stayed with Amado and his wife, writer Zélia Gattai. At their welcoming home Seghers wrote under the shade of a tree in the garden. She sailed back to Europe alone, László Radványi electing to fly this time. Once she was back in Berlin she said she felt "landsick" and missed the life at sea.

In the GDR Seghers's thoughts often turned to the continent that granted her asylum. Much of her GDR writing is set in Latin America and the Caribbean, including short stories and novellas such as *Crisanta* (1951), *Caribbean Stories*

(1948/ 1961), *Benito's Blue* (1967) and her last short book, *Three Women from Haiti* (1980). *Crossing* (1971) has a transitional setting aboard a ship. The narrative begins as the *Norwid* leaves Santos, and ends before it reaches Rostock. The story depicts a journey home across the ocean from south to north, from west to east, perhaps reflected in the four main stars of the Southern Cross constellation. *Crossing* is not only testament to Seghers's supreme skill as a storyteller, it also affords the attentive reader much insight into the life and views of this great international, onetime exiled, writer, whose work contains as a central recurring theme the search for home.

The Visit
(1956, extract)

We sat on our still-to-be-unpacked suitcases covered in travel labels from every country and continent imaginable, the only appealing signs of color in the bleak room. We had often sat like this in the intervening years on these same suitcases, in some foreign city or other, four or five companions-in-exile. We had just arrived in Berlin. We were home.

For years we had imagined our return home. We constantly pictured our country while on the run or in uncertain asylum, on ships in the war or in bombed cities, amidst ruins and in books that others (or we ourselves) had written. Time and again, the power of our imaginations had brought to life anew that which was dear to us.

Now we sat silently together. One of us was telling how he had finally managed to make it home at the last moment. Our conversation subsided. But no angel went through the room. It was more an anxious silence. We saw even clearer the cracks in the walls, the windowpanes stuck with paper. Through window remains we looked onto the ruins. The ruined city merged with the evening sky, as though it still smoldered and smoked.

The people we passed on the street looked vacant, sad, and forlorn; embittered by their misery; above all by the thought that they themselves had caused it. Far away we had longed for our language—it had become harsh and grating. We had put words together so that we never lost the sound of it; it had eased our homesickness—now it hurt to be home. In our memories, our native land had flourished—now in reality it was bleak and drab. That is what we thought then, in that dreary hotel room.

— Anna Seghers, 1956; 'The Visit' in *Über Kunstwerk und Wirklichkeit. Für den Frieden der Welt*, vol. 3, ed. by Sigrid Bock (Berlin: Akademie Verlag, 1971) 164-5.

Translator Douglas Irving is from Scotland, UK. In the 1990s he studied Spanish and German at Aberdeen University, where he first encountered *Überfahrt: Eine Liebesgeschichte*. In 2013/4 he obtained a Masters in Translation Studies at Glasgow University, and began to translate Anna Seghers's 1971 novel.